Praise for Idra Novey's

WAYS TO DISAPPEAR

Winner of the Brooklyn Eagles Literary Prize

"An elegant page-turner.... This lush and tightly woven novel manages to be a meditation on all forms of translation while still charging forward with the momentum of a bullet.... Novey writes with cool precision and breakneck pacing."
— Catherine Lacey, *New York Times Book Review*

"Bewitching.... A tale of playful suspense that ingeniously transmutes into a profound meditation on language and love."
— Elliott Holt, *O, The Oprah Magazine*

"Reminiscent of a Coen brothers movie.... A spare, witty riddle of a novel." — Sam Sacks, *Wall Street Journal*

"Exhilarating.... Sly, lovely.... In Raquel, Beatriz's hard-bitten daughter, Novey has created a heartrending portrait of the price someone always ends up paying for genius. A writer to watch."
— Charles Finch, *USA Today*

"Novey's fleet and vivid novel examines the nature of personal agency in life and in fiction, challenging the notion that we 'honor what we recall by accepting that we cannot change it.'"
— *The New Yorker*

"Uniquely captivating.... An immensely entertaining read."
— Margie Romero, *Pittsburgh Post-Gazette*

"Idra Novey, an acclaimed poet and translator of Spanish and Portuguese literature, has written a debut novel that's a fast-paced, beguilingly playful, noirish literary mystery with a translator at its center. *Ways to Disappear* explores the meaning behind a writer's words—the way they can both hide and reveal deep truths.... Novey's novel delivers on its promises in so many ways. Yes, there's carnage, but there's also exuberant love, revelations of long-buried, unhappy secrets, ruminations about what makes a satisfying life, a publisher's regrets about moral compromises in both his work and his use of his family wealth and connections, and an alternately heartfelt and wry portrait of the satisfactions and anxieties of the generally underappreciated art of translation.... *Ways to Disappear* is concerned not just with truth and the risks of its misplacement and misinterpretation, but with the importance of close reading. It's a delightful, inventive paean to writing.... This book is seared to perfection."

— Heller McAlpin, NPR.org

"Novey is astute, funny, and cunning in this story, which even in its brevity covers so much lush ground."

— Meredith Turits, Elle.com

"A seductive mystery.... Novey brings to her first novel a zesty comic touch and refreshing insights into the delicate processes of writing and translation."

— Jane Ciabattari, BBC

"A fun, entertaining story.... Novey uses a light, sensitive touch and a giddy sense of play to explore weighty concepts...in a novel whose powers of enchantment rival those of its fictional author."

— Anita Felicelli, *San Francisco Chronicle*

"Idra Novey is an enchantress. Her sentences are so surprising and beautiful, her vision of the world so kaleidoscopic, that I fell immediately and permanently under the spell of this glorious novel." —Karen Russell, author of *Vampires in the Lemon Grove*

"In Idra Novey's delightful debut novel, *Ways to Disappear,* language is a fascinating plot all by itself.... Novey's fascination with language and writing allows her to draw multiple meanings from every turn.... Keywords such as *promise, permission,* and *matter* receive the dictionary treatment, allowing moments just described to resonate in clever, often haunting, ways. Each one is like a poem." —Katherine Hill, *Philadelphia Inquirer*

"Novey writes elegantly and with slanted humor about beauty, loss, abandonment, and surprising acts of self-discovery.... The three main characters embark on a hot pursuit that mimics pulp fiction on its caperish exterior, but literary fiction in its deep center.... With touches of mystery, commentary about the art of translating as well as inventing fiction, prose that reads like poetry, and snatches of actual poems, *Ways to Disappear* is a gem." —Jeffrey Ann Goudie, *Kansas City Star*

"Exceptionally witty *and* heartfelt is not the usual combo. Nothing about this novel is usual. Every sentence surprises. Every character intrigues. I read this book with joy and serious admiration." —Amy Bloom, author of *Lucky Us*

"Idra Novey has created something special with the brisk, beautiful *Ways to Disappear,* a book that blooms in the spaces between languages, between continents, between selves past and present." —Dustin Illingworth, *Los Angeles Times*

"Poet and translator Idra Novey brings a considerable imagination to her first work of fiction.... Stylish and funny, romantic and surreal, *Ways to Disappear* is a quirky look at the intimate relationship between author and translator.... Though *Ways to Disappear* unfolds at the rapid pace of a screwball comedy, there is also something patient and artful about the novel, making it a thoughtful treatise on writing and artmaking that is as profound as it is playful."
—Lauren Bufferd, *BookPage*

"Sensual and fast-paced, suspenseful and subtle, full of observations about Brazilian life and North American double standards.... Action-packed."
—Marta Bausells, *The Guardian*

"Exciting, romantic, and deceptively simple."
—Joseph Peschel, *St. Louis Post-Dispatch*

"Using her poet's—and translator's—precision, Novey seeds her story with crystalline images, like perfect little dioramas through which her characters move.... Novey has crafted a delightfully metafictional and metatranslational exploration into the creation and appreciation of literature."
—Ashley Patronyak, *Bookslut*

"With tremendous intelligence and wit, *Ways to Disappear* upends all the misleading memes about magical realism and in the process makes its own very real and unprecedented magic. This is a fantastic book."
—Rivka Galchen, author of *Atmospheric Disturbances*

"A fun, compulsively readable, consistently refreshing adventure."
—Sarah Gerard, *Hazlitt*

"Novey has a knack for engaging, humorous prose and audacious plotting the likes of which are rarely seen in a first novel."

—Jonathon Sturgeon, *Flavorwire*

"*Ways to Disappear* defies convention and categorization, effortlessly careening from magical realism to noir, reckless romance to metafictional dictionary definitions. The result is a story as propulsive as it is compelling. Virtually unputdownable."

—Jim Ruland, *Los Angeles Review of Books*

"Idra Novey's debut novel cast me under its spell from the opening scene.... *Ways to Disappear* reads like a thriller and scores thematically on the missteps of translation and the untenable distances of the heart." —Amy Jo Burns, *Ploughshares*

"Compelling and strange and wonderfully perfect.... You can disappear for hours in Novey's original story."

—Nina Schuyler, *The Rumpus*

"Novey's characters are hilariously impulsive, terribly misguided, hopelessly lost, relentlessly determined, and immediately sympathetic. An incisive meditation on the relationship between literature and life, a reflection on the cumulative result of everyday decisions, and a dazzling, truly memorable work of humor and heart." —*Booklist*

"At once playful and chilling. It's impossible to put this book down, or to shake its residue once you've finished it."

—Leslie Jamison, author of *The Empathy Exams*

"Fast-paced and colorful, *Ways to Disappear* is part mystery, part romance, but 100 percent a delight." —Jarry Lee, *Buzzfeed*

"*Ways to Disappear* is a thoughtful tropical noir with depth and feeling. . . . Full of gorgeously rendered action. . . . Novey's prose is surprising, working its magic without ostentation in a way that makes the best lines feel like joyful ambushes."
—Zachary C. Solomon, *Full Stop*

"Written in short poetic chapters and punctuated with dictionary definitions, *Ways to Disappear* is both a meditation on the art of translation and a classic mystery complete with loan sharks, amateur detectives, and an ill-advised romance."
—Emma Brown, *Interview*

"A comic, noirish page-turner and a clever, metafictional reflection on the nature of translating."
—Francesca Angelini, *The Times* (UK)

"Stylish, absurd, sometimes romantic, and often very funny. . . . Like a dream, the book is almost overwhelmingly vivid. . . . It's a tour de force. Delightful and original."   —*Kirkus Reviews*

"A supercharged and perfectly timed novel."
—Jeva Lange, *Electric Literature*

"This amazing first novel is unlike any other you've ever read. *Ways to Disappear* is a lush page-turner, a journey into the unique madness of modern Brazil, and a joyful ride into the crazed passion of literary creation itself. Idra Novey is a wonder of a writer."
—Héctor Tobar, author of *Deep Down Dark*

"A clever literary mystery and a playful portrait of the artist as a young translator—it reads like an Ali Smith novel with a fun Brazilian-noir vibe."   —*Publishers Weekly*

"Novey, an accomplished poet and translator, sustains suspense throughout with beautifully restrained prose. Yet her narrative is more than a mystery—it's about language itself, both the yearning for comprehension and the desire to feel understood."

—Carmela Ciuraru, *New York Times*

"Spare, funny, and moving. How can a novel so elegant and blazingly smart be so much fun?"

—Ted Thompson, author of *The Land of Steady Habits*

"Novey's debut has a warmth and humor all her own.... A novel that will leave you in a glow."

—Lauren Goldenberg, *Music & Literature*

"With all its shimmering brilliance and insight, vividly drawn and beguiling characters, and unabashed storytelling, *Ways to Disappear* is the most sublime novel I've read in a long time."

—Francisco Goldman, author of *Say Her Name*

"An experimental page-turner.... It's got both Borgesian meta ness and García Márquez's magical realism in its DNA.... It's a canny mystery brimming with stories and pithy observations about the world of literature."
—JoAnna Novak, *Bustle*

"Idra Novey has given us a first-rate novel of ideas, a book that is also funny, poignant, and profound."

—Darcey Steinke, author of *Sister Golden Hair*

ALSO BY IDRA NOVEY

Poetry

Exit, Civilian

The Next Country

Translations

The Passion According to G.H. by Clarice Lispector

On Elegance While Sleeping by Viscount Lascano Tegui

Birds for a Demolition by Manoel de Barros

The Clean Shirt of It by Paulo Henriques Britto

WAYS TO DISAPPEAR

A Novel

Idra Novey

BACK BAY BOOKS

Little, Brown and Company

New York • Boston • London

Back Bay Books / Little, Brown and Company
Hachette Book Group
1290 Avenue of the Americas, New York, NY 10104
littlebrown.com

Originally published in hardcover by Little, Brown and Company, February 2016
First Back Bay paperback edition, January 2017

Back Bay Books is an imprint of Little, Brown and Company, a division of Hachette Book Group, Inc. The Back Bay Books name and logo are trademarks of Hachette Book Group, Inc.

The publisher is not responsible for websites (or their content) that are not owned by the publisher.

The Hachette Speakers Bureau provides a wide range of authors for speaking events. To find out more, go to hachettespeakersbureau.com or call (866) 376-6591.

ISBN 978-0-316-29849-0 (hardcover) / 978-0-316-29847-6 (paperback)
LCCN 2015942285

For Leo, for every coast with you

For a time we became the same word. It could not last.
— Edmond Jabès
Translated by Rosmarie Waldrop

WAYS TO DISAPPEAR

In a crumbling park in the crumbling back end of Copacabana, a woman stopped under an almond tree with a suitcase and a cigar. She was a round woman with a knob of gray hair pinned at the nape of her neck. After staring for a minute up into the tree, she bit into her cigar, lifted her suitcase onto the lowest branch, and climbed up after it.

Would you look at that, one of the domino players in the park said as the woman climbed higher, exposing the frayed elastic of her cotton underwear and the dimpled undersides of her thighs.

The domino players were about to break for lunch but didn't think it was right to leave a woman sitting in an almond tree with a cigar and a suitcase. Julio, the ladies' man, was selected to investigate. To prepare for the task, he gave a pinch to the tips of his mustache and checked the alignment of his suspenders. At the base of the tree, he looked up and found the woman's ample behind looming directly over his head. To see the rest of her, he had to shuffle over a step and saw that she had opened a book across her lap as if she were sitting at a train station.

Senhora, could I be of assistance? he asked.

The woman thanked him for inquiring but said she'd been looking forward to this day for some time and was perched there so serenely with her open book and cigar that Julio wished her well and he went home for some beans.

Over rice and beans in front of the TV, the Portuguese translator Emma Neufeld told her boyfriend that she was nervous. Her author hadn't answered her emails in over a week.

Miles told her she spent too much time fretting over unanswered emails. His preferred subject of late was when they might get married, and whether they had to invite everyone in their Road Runners group. He said he was leaning toward an outside venue regardless.

Emma, on the other hand, was leaning toward never.

She had yet to express this.

That evening, an email finally arrived from Brazil but it was not from Beatriz. The sender said his name was Flamenguinho. Was Senhora Neufeld aware, the man inquired, that her author had recently climbed into an almond tree with a suitcase and hadn't been seen in the five days since then?

Emma drew closer to the screen to make sure she'd read the message correctly. She murmured the words in Portuguese for *almond tree* and *suitcase*. For *author* and *disappear*. On the shelf in front of her stood the five works of translation that had consumed her life since graduate school. She'd finished one after another with the intensity of an addict. No other translator, in any language, had published as many works by Beatriz.

Downstairs, Miles had begun the nightly preparations for their early run tomorrow. She heard the thump of their sneakers as he placed them by the door, the clink of her keys as he positioned them beside her banana. To leave a person capable of such meticulous devotion was difficult.

She clicked to the weather. Outside their rented, somewhat shabby house in Pittsburgh, it was snowing sideways. In Rio de Janeiro, it was 106 degrees.

On the phone, Raquel Yagoda told her mother's translator there was no reason for Emma to come to Brazil. It isn't necessary, she said, and you don't want to be in the heat wave we're having now.

Emma continued to insist, however, until Raquel apologized and said that she had to get off the phone. On TV Globo, the news was flashing the same ancient photographs over and over: her mother in a purple polyester pantsuit receiving the Jabuti Prize in 1983, her mother seven months pregnant with Marcus at the book festival in Porto Alegre, her mother in a TV interview when her hair was still dark and thick and her body so thin she folded shut like a fan when she swiveled in a chair.

If you have any information about the South African writer Beatriz Yagoda, the newscaster said, please call the number below.

South African, Raquel repeated, and clicked off the TV. Her mother had left Johannesburg when she was two. Her mother was about as South African as bossa nova.

By the time they reached the Pittsburgh airport, Emma was thinking in Portuguese. Beside her, Miles went on exploding in English about what an unnecessary escapade this trip was. It's so impulsive, he said, when we have a wedding to pay for.

Emma let him blast on. She was tired of explaining. She didn't just know Beatriz's books. She knew the melon color of her author's bathrobe and which side of the sofa Beatriz preferred when she curled up to read. For the last seven years, Emma had been making an annual pilgrimage with her yearly stipend for language research to see her author. She planned the trips well in advance, and Miles had never given her a hard time about them. He'd never asked much about them either, which she'd come to appreciate. Having never reduced the trips to anecdotes, she could recall them more intuitively as she worked on her translations. She'd remember a morning in Rio as no more than an orange glow over the ocean and use that light to illuminate the strange, dark boats of Beatriz's images as she ferried them into English.

Miles was wrong. She knew Beatriz too intimately not to go and help now. What if no one else thought of the scene in one of Beatriz's earliest stories with the warden who disappears into a tree? Emma couldn't recall the title of it with Miles continuing to detonate beside her in the car. But she was certain that she'd remember it once she was alone in the airport.

And indeed, in the security line, the title came to her. "A Lua Nova." The New Moon. Once she'd recalled the name, she remembered the whole story, the island with nothing on it but a prison and an orchestra of three-toed lizards that serenade the inmates each night with samba and *maracatu*. The story was about a mute inmate who whittled chicken bones and the warden who fell in love with him and then poisoned the prisoner, hoping that would extinguish his longing.

But there was a second warden in the story, too. A minor character who climbed a palm tree outside the walls to listen to the lizards and found the distance so freeing, sitting there elevated and unseen, away from the other wardens and their prisoners, that he never came down.

Or maybe there was a suggestion that something more happened in the tree — Emma couldn't remember. She'd have to find the story when she got to Beatriz's apartment. If not, the friend who'd been kind enough to write to her about her author's disappearance would surely have a copy of the collection. Beatriz had never mentioned anyone named Flamenguinho, but he clearly knew Beatriz well enough to know how close she was to Emma. He knew what an asset her American translator would be in a crisis like this. They were going to meet for drinks at Emma's hotel as soon as she landed. She was so eager to feel the honeyed lilt of Portuguese in her mouth again, the breeze off the Atlantic on her skin.

When she finally emerged from Rio's Galeão International Airport, she took in the familiar stink of armpits, car exhaust, and guavas that assaulted her as she stepped out of the baggage claim and the outside air pressed in. Already she could feel her dress adhering to her arms and lower back. After so much winter, the sticky sensation, the rising odors were glorious. To arrive in Rio was to remember that one had a body and brought it everywhere.

Her cabdriver had a body as well, much of it on display beneath his pink muscle shirt, all of it glistening with sweat. When he asked her where she'd learned Portuguese, she told him about Beatriz.

But you must want to translate the real greats, he said, masters like Jorge Amado and Carlos Drummond.

So she told him about the warden in the tree, the island prison with its night orchestra of lizards, how it was one of those stories so strange and spare that it felt like a whispered, secret history of the world.

Oh, I know it. The Devil's Cauldron, the driver said.

No, I believe she called it "The New Moon," Emma replied.

I'm talking about the prison, he said. It gets hot as a pot of hell there on Ilha Grande.

Ilha what? I can't understand your accent.

Flamenguinho let out a belch so explosive his eyes bulged like a toad's. At the eruption, several people at the bar turned around slack-jawed. Emma couldn't imagine Beatriz seeking out the company of such a man. Besides his belching problem, he had what appeared to be a tattoo of a trash can on his neck.

He also kept posing his questions to her breasts. Who's helping her on Ilha Grande? he asked her shirt.

Well, I think it has more to do with this early story of hers, Emma said. It takes place on —

Rerp! Another belch detonated, and with such force that Flamenguinho had to grab hold of the table.

Listen, he said to her breasts, fuck the story. You know what I want? I want the six hundred thousand fucking dollars she owes me. Okay? I know she's broke. So you need to get the damn book from her. Whatever you get for it in your country, half a million is mine, and then I won't have to kill her.

Emma looked down at her hands. Her fingers had come together in what her yoga teachers called the bind. It didn't seem like the time to explain that Elsewhere Press was just a woman named Judie in upstate New York and various interns from a small university nearby. For each book Judie published, she'd paid Emma the same amount she'd paid Beatriz: five hundred dollars. To make a living, Emma taught endless sections of "Portuguese for Spanish Speakers" at a branch campus of the University of Pittsburgh.

Her fingers still bound, she asked Flamenguinho how he'd gotten hold of her email, and he flared his nostrils.

See this? He opened his jacket to reveal the gun-shaped bulge in the left inside pocket. It would be deadly, he said, for you to assume I'm an idiot. I found you online like any other asshole, and if you sell her book and send me the money I won't have to find you again. You hear what I'm saying?

Beset with a slight sensation of vertigo, Emma nodded. Of the various scenarios in which she'd imagined herself in Rio, receiving a threat of this nature was not one of them. She'd also never imagined her author as someone who would conceal an addiction, and certainly not to gambling. She'd translated every emotion Beatriz had ever written. They'd discussed hundreds of words and why Beatriz had chosen them over others. They'd sipped coffee together in their pajamas. Emma had gradually come to trust her understanding of her author's impulses more than she did her own. If she couldn't find Beatriz, she couldn't find anyone.

I think I have an idea of where she might be, Emma told the shark sitting before her. If she's finished the book, I'll translate it as fast as I can. Whatever it makes in the U.S. is yours. I promise.

Promise: From the late Middle English *prom-is.* First known use 15th century. **1.** A declaration of what a person intends to do, which may correspond to what a person actually does, or may not. **2.** A verb used to assure of a certain outcome, as in: *With time, a translator gets used to promising the impossible the way a loan shark gets used to promising carnage.* **See also:** humanity after Babel, hangings during the Inquisition, chamber music in the dark.

Raquel let her brother open the door for Emma. She hadn't wanted to deal with her mother's translator yet, but Marcus said that Emma had come such a long way to help them. If she was eager to speak to them, they really couldn't say no.

Raquel didn't agree, but then she'd never understood why her mother let Emma stay in the guest room. A translator wasn't family and her mother never referred to Emma as a friend. Yet every June her mother's translator arrived, and so thin and high-strung it was impossible to relax when she was in the apartment. Her sunscreen was a problem, too. During Emma's visits, the living room would begin to reek of those American lotions with an excess of zinc.

The story about the obese loan shark with the burps was just the sort of paranoid nonsense Emma would provide. A psychologist friend of her mother's had already told them what must have happened. Her mother had suffered a sudden onset of amnesia or was in the throes of a dissociative fugue. How else to explain why a woman in her sixties would drag a suitcase into a tree?

Sure, her mother had always liked poker and liked to win. She often played poker games with them as children, and real games with her writer friends as well. In either case, she never gave away what sort of cards she was holding until the hand was over.

But her mother would never have played online, and for serious money. She'd never had serious money, and if a loan shark had observed what a good player her mother was and goaded her to raise the stakes with his money, her mother wouldn't have risked it. What for? Her mother had a whole clan of elderly aunts in São Paulo who wired her cash whenever she needed it, although the calls had their cost, too. They always ended with her mother hunched over and apologizing, saying, You're right, you're right, that's what I should've done.

As a teenager, Raquel had often made the calls for her. Each time, the aunts would recount the same story about her mother falling out of a tree as a child and hitting her head, how it explained everything. Still, the aunts always sent more than her mother requested. If her mother called too close to Shabbat, they wired the money first thing on Monday.

This man was making a joke of you, Raquel said to Emma.

He had a gun in his jacket.

Half the people in Rio have guns in their jackets, don't they, Marcus? Raquel turned to her brother, but he'd taken a seat at their mother's desk and was brushing aside various chocolate wrappers and crumpled napkins to find the keyboard.

Don't turn on her computer, Raquel said. Leave it alone. She would never have gambled online. If she was on her computer, she was writing.

Marcus turned it on.

Until she met them, Emma hadn't given much thought to the fact that her author had children. On her first visit to Brazil, she'd been caught off guard by the sight of a young man in the living room with the same radioactive-green eyes and high cheekbones as Beatriz. Marcus's gaze, however, had none of his mother's intensity. His stare was sensual and sleepy. Several nights a week, he tended bar at one of the most expensive clubs in Leblon, where, Emma had not been surprised to learn, he received such extraordinary tips he had no motivation to pursue anything else.

His older sister was the one who'd inherited their mother's intensity, but on Raquel's face it had worked out differently. Her eyes were small and suspicious, her default expression one of displeasure. When Emma first met her, Raquel had been furious about the unions she dealt with at a large mining company. Now she was at an even larger mining company and even more furious about the unions there.

One night, after they'd sat talking for hours on the balcony, Emma had asked Beatriz if she'd made a deliberate point of not writing about her children. Beatriz had looked at her with confusion and said the novel Emma had just translated was all about them. Emma had blushed and said of course, she meant earlier, in other books.

Once Beatriz said it, the parallels between the mayors in the novel and her offspring were obvious. *Have You Tasted the Butterflies* followed the fates of two mayors running adjacent towns along the Amazon River. One of the mayors was industrious and continually repainting and rebuilding the docks to draw in tourists and their dollars. Regardless of what he improved, all the foreigners who came down the river stopped at the town of the other mayor, who rebuilt nothing and shrugged at the problem of townspeople tossing their trash along the riverbank. The rotting piles attracted vultures and thousands of mosquitoes but also great clusters of pink and orange butterflies that landed in fluttering clouds on the arms of travelers who would stand on the broken docks, gasping at the tickle of so many pink wings beating against their skin.

To compete, the industrious mayor planted milkweed and bought vats of caterpillars from various hatcheries. Yet the minute his butterflies emerged, they flickered off to the trash heaps along the banks of the other mayor's town.

Puta que o pariu, Marcus swore at his mother's screen. Emma took a quiet step closer to see what he had opened. It was his mother's Web history, riddled with poker sites.

Let me see that. Raquel pushed her brother to get up and surrender control of the keyboard.

Maybe I should go, Emma said.

No, no, please don't. Marcus stood up, motioning for her to follow him into the kitchen and leave Raquel to click through the Web history on her own. From the fruit bowl on the kitchen counter he extracted some old lemons, clenched them, and shrugged.

We'll make do, he said, and began to prepare a trio of caipirinhas, compensating for the limits of the lemons with extra cachaça and sugar. When he handed Emma her glass, he paused to watch her lips close over the rim.

There's no reason for you to pay for a hotel, he said. My mother liked for you to stay here. The guest room is yours if you want it.

Emma had every intention of being respectful. She wanted to leave every object in her author's bathroom precisely where it was when she arrived. With Beatriz in the next room, it had never occurred to her to pick up her author's matted brush and run it through her own hair. Only now Beatriz was not in the next room, and once Emma allowed herself to pick up her author's brush and pull it through her hair, it became necessary to do it again, and then a third time.

Outside the bathroom, the apartment was so quiet she could hear the thrum of cars along Rua Barata Ribeiro, or perhaps it was something closer: the persimmons and *maracujá* softening in the kitchen, or the murmur of her author's books on the shelves, questioning when she might return.

On her last trip to Brazil, Emma had stood next to Beatriz just outside this bathroom and confessed that she hadn't been quite as dutiful in her last translation as in Beatriz's earlier books, and Beatriz had replied that duty was for clergy. For translation to be an art, she told Emma, you have to make the uncomfortable but necessary transgressions that an artist makes.

With Beatriz gone, what might qualify as a necessary transgression was even less clear. In coming to Brazil in her author's absence, she had put herself on trial. In the bathroom mirror,

Emma stared at the reflection of her hand, the brush in it that was not hers but to whose bristles she had just added a layer of her hair. In her mind, a medieval courtroom appeared. The walls were made of stones and her view was from the stand. Dozens of spectators were squinting at her, and looking down at herself, she saw why. Her hands and arms had turned hazy at the edges. Her legs, too. When she reached up to touch her face, it was like passing her hand through vapor. Yet everyone in the gallery was staring in her direction. They could see her, or at least found her legible enough to be tried for her alleged crimes.

Emma tried to think from what book or movie she could be recalling such an odd court scene. Unless perhaps the image hadn't come from elsewhere and was hers, something she'd been storing up for some time but hadn't been able to recognize as her own until she found herself alone in this apartment and had lifted this brush to her hair. Until she'd heard the snap of her own strands trapped in its bristles.

Raquel picked up her phone to call her boss then decided against it. Thiago had become more than her boss in the nine years they'd been working together, but how much more varied unpredictably. To call him when she was this upset could be a mistake. He might think she couldn't handle the brutes running the strike up in Minas and he'd give the negotiations to Enrico.

She sat down on her bed. She could always call Marcus but knew she'd hang up feeling lonelier. They'd just disagree again and most likely he was already on the ferry with Emma. Raquel objected to the trip. She'd admitted that she didn't have any better ideas about where to search, but that was no reason to take a trip based on some story her mother had written twenty years ago. Emma was like all her mother's pretentious admirers who thought they had a special understanding of her mother because they'd studied her books. But they knew nothing of her mother's days in bed after calling the aunts in São Paulo for rent money or occasionally for no reason her mother could name. She'd just go on lying there, still as a crocodile with her reptilian-green eyes, listening if Raquel spoke, but unwilling, or unable, to answer.

If her mother was hiding on an island, Raquel was certain it would be one much farther away. Ilha Grande was too close to Rio and full of bourgeois bohemians. Her mother wouldn't want to be surrounded by a bunch of bobos in flip-flops smoking pot while they texted on their iPhones. The government had dynamited the prison years ago. Raquel had watched the explosion on the news with her mother. As the prison fell, her mother had pointed out the birds flapping upward out of the trees and said, Look, the birds are collapsing into the sky. Raquel had looked reluctantly for the birds through the smoke. She would have liked to have spoken with her mother just once about what was actually happening. A demolition.

When people asked what it was like to be the daughter of someone who came up with such peculiar stories, Raquel told them the truth. She'd never read her mother's books. She had no patience for the illusion that you could know someone because you knew her novels. What about knowing what a writer had never written down—wasn't that the real knowledge of who she was?

True to the nature of public transportation in Brazil, the ferry to Ilha Grande was running an hour late. Emma, true to the nature of anxious travelers everywhere, took the opportunity to head to the nearest Internet café. Her inbox contained two messages from Miles but she didn't open them. She'd paid for only ten minutes and wanted to search for the genus of toad she'd discussed with Marcus in the cab. In English it was called the red-belly.

> **Scientific name:** *Melanophryniscus montevidensis.*

> **In Brazilian Portuguese:** *Flamenguinho,* after the Rio de Janeiro soccer team Flamengo, its colors red and black.

> **Toxic alkaloid/poison level:** Highly variable, often fatal.

The esteemed literary publisher Roberto Rocha liked to test his steaks to see if the meat was worth what he had paid for it. The test had to do with the density of the smoke once the steaks began to sizzle. With the works of fiction he selected for his press, he tested for density as well, for something tender in the middle yet still heavy enough to blacken the air.

He had not come across such a manuscript in years. Everything that appeared in the stack on his desk bored him within the first forty pages. Even the works he agreed to publish struck him as cheap, dry cuts now, something synthetic in their flavor. He wished someone had warned him that devoting his life and inheritance to a literary press would leave him this overweight and cynical. Of course, if they had, he would have written off that person as an imbecile and a philistine.

Senhor Roberto? His assistant, Flavia, knocked on the door and ducked her head in. The mail came. There's a letter from your cousin Luisa.

That's nice, he said, since I don't have a cousin named Luisa.

Maybe it says Laura Flaks. Or Lourdes? The handwriting is a little odd. Flavia pushed up the thick dark-rimmed glasses all the literary girls wore now and handed him the envelope.

The surname Flaks did ring a bell, though not for anyone in his family. Rocha was fairly certain it was Jewish.

Caro Roberto, the letter began, I hate to ask this, but I hope that given the circumstances, you would be kind enough to help a cousin in a hard spot hide out for a week at the hotel below.

How perfectly bizarre, Rocha said.

And then it came to him: the bubble bath scene in the opening pages of the novel that had put his press on the map. Luisa Flaks with her head back, her long wet hair spread out like a spider web against the porcelain of the tub. Sensual, ordinary Luisa reclining in the bath, or not quite ordinary, as she'd had the nerve to resist turning off the faucets, had let the water spill steadily over the edge of the tub and across the tiles and seep into the apartment below, had let the spill go on until her skin had shriveled at the center of her fingertips and her toes and she could no longer feel her backbone against the porcelain. Rocha had been concerned that the scene was too extreme, that the descriptions dragged on too long, but Beatriz had insisted that was the point: to push everything—the amount of water, the details. To take all of it too far.

The novel had been the only book Rocha had ever published that went into a second printing within a month. After her next book won every major award in Brazil, he'd encouraged Beatriz to leave his press for a larger, international house. He hadn't wanted to hold her back. He'd hoped she might continue to share her drafts with him, and she had. Every one.

In the other desk, he said to Flavia, is my checkbook. Would you bring it here?

A light rain began to slant across the deck as Emma boarded the ferry. Despite the drizzle, two boys by the prow were taking out a pair of battered-looking guitars. Others, including Marcus, had taken advantage of the benches under the roof to stretch out and nap through the ride.

Emma was too exhilarated to rest. She sat down at the end of the long bench where Marcus was sleeping so she could keep watch over his bag. Pittsburgh, Miles, her job—all of it felt like a skin she'd shed on the plane. Even English and who she was in it felt discardable, or at least until the long-haired boys at the prow began strumming the chords to "Redemption Song." A girl with a necklace made of brightly painted beans started to sing the lyrics. Before long, a whole group was crooning "No Woman, No Cry" at a decibel and tenor that were impossible to tune out.

Emma turned to share her dismay with Marcus, but his eyes were closed. All across the open deck, people were making pillows out of each other's laps. The rain was blowing more sharply now, and Marcus had stretched out along the bench in such a way that his head was nearly touching her bare knee.

She tried to slide down to a more appropriate distance but Marcus just stretched out longer, moving toward her in his sleep, or perhaps it was more intentional.

What she did know was that no 10K run with Miles would ever lead to a ferry ride in a mist like this. The thought arrived just as Marcus tipped his face back, his full, soft mouth so close she could feel his breath against her thigh. When something flashed brightly off to her left, she thought, Lightning.

Bom dia, Brazil!

Here at Radio Globo we like to get the morning rolling with some news about love, and Rio's new heartthrob, Marcus Yagoda, has found it, my friends, in the arms of his mother's translator. The still-missing author was a sizzler once herself and we've got the photos to prove it at globo.com.

Why her son was seen on a ferry off to holiday on Ilha Grande instead of looking for his mother in the trees of her fair city, we don't know. But let's wish him well, my friends. He is a son in strange waters, which seems as good a reason as any to fall in love.

Raquel opened the newspaper to the gossip page to look at it again. She'd gone out earlier for some fresh *pão de queijo* but had no desire to eat now. In the photograph, the rain and low gray sky over the ferry made her brother and Emma look like refu-gees fleeing a civil war, surviving a storm on passion alone.

Raquel had texted Marcus ten times, though she knew he wasn't likely to be awake yet. With all the press their mother was getting, he should've considered that there might be a journalist on the ferry, and to fall asleep on Emma's lap that way was bound to result in a headline like South African Author Still Missing, Son Rests on Her Translator.

She'd seen enough women gaze at her brother's face to know what would happen next. By tomorrow morning, the two of them would be searching for Emma's underwear in the hotel sheets instead of searching the island. They weren't going to find her mother there, but regardless, it was the reason they'd left Raquel here to sit panicking alone over the bounced checks and overdraft fees multiplying with each mail delivery. The debt was far beyond anything they'd ever asked the aunts in São Paulo to cover, and Raquel couldn't bear to call and hear what they would say.

This morning, before the paper arrived, she'd broken into her mother's online poker accounts. It hadn't taken long to figure out the password. Their mother used the same combination of birth dates for everything. The amount of money her mother had bet and lost was staggering. It had gone on for over two years, and most of the loss was under the name O Sapateiro, the Shoemaker—what her mother's father had become when the money he'd brought from Johannesburg ran out. Raquel could remember sitting in his shop, watching him stare mystified at his own tools. In South Africa, he'd been a lawyer, but his limited Portuguese had made that impossible in Brazil.

Now his daughter had created an even more impossible situation. Reading through the mounting losses in her mother's accounts, Raquel felt a shrinking inside her. She should've gone ahead and called Thiago yesterday. Now it was Saturday and she couldn't. He would be with his wife and their sons. She'd followed him to PetroXM, thinking that they'd have an affair eventually, but Thiago seemed too decent for that, or feared she would be the type of woman who would push him to leave his family, and he would be right. She would.

She wanted him here now, slurping a beer beside her, spewing vulgar jokes about her mother's poker skills, jokes that were so outrageous that she would be laughing despite herself. Even Thiago would have known to lay off when the amount of money lost passed half a million and her mother hadn't stopped. In a panic, or goaded by Flamenguinho to recover his investment, her mother had gone on playing as if gambling online were no more than a tale she had invented, as if she were still a child and didn't know the difference, still the daughter who made up ghost stories for her father while he resoled the boots of strangers.

The thought filled Raquel with resentment and longing. It

was like sitting in the hot car again, waiting for her mother to return. Once, the wait had been treacherously long. The temperature in the car had gone on rising until she felt dizzy, the hot seat painful against her skin. Her eyes kept getting drier, her thoughts blurring in her head. When her mother finally rushed up to the car, sweaty and upset and apologetic, Raquel assumed she'd gotten lost. Her mother didn't explain, and Raquel had been too afraid to ask.

Marcus jumped up from the table. That was her, he said. That was my mother. I'm sure of it.

The rain was shattering down outside the restaurant as if someone had smashed a glass pitcher. Marcus ran into it anyway, and Emma felt obliged to follow. The first two times he'd been convinced he'd seen his mother on the island, both women had turned out to be tourists from Germany. Now, around the corner, Marcus and Emma startled a small freckled woman from Australia.

I'm sorry, Marcus said as they returned to their table, water dripping down their foreheads into their eyes.

It's okay. It's hard to see in this rain. Emma mopped her face with one of the napkins from the dispenser on the table, but it was futile. Like the napkins in all cheap Brazilian restaurants, they were plastic-based and made her feel like she was wiping her face with a garbage bag. She had lost her stamina for startling foreigners in the rain. If Beatriz was on this island, it was going to be on the other side, where the ruins of the prison were, and where none of the boatmen would take them until the storm passed.

I'm getting cold, she told Marcus. Don't you want to put on some dry clothes?

I don't mind. You go ahead. I'll keep looking.

She nodded, swatting at the mosquitoes feasting on her ankles. She hoped she'd get a respite from them in her room, but the mosquitoes were there as well, sneaking in through the holes in the window screens and between the planks of the floor. The only place to avoid them was under the grimy netting draped over the bed. Trapped beneath it, scratching at her bites, Emma opened the various books she'd brought to read but was too itchy to get into any of them.

She pulled out her notebook. The courtroom scene that had come to her in Beatriz's bathroom had continued to return. Each time, her mind took her a little further into the scene and the images wouldn't let go of her until she'd written them down. She didn't know if she was embarrassing herself by taking the scene seriously enough to record it, but what did she have to lose? She was so good and humiliated already, having insisted on this trip to Ilha Grande with such confidence that she'd led her author's son to believe finding his mother might just be a matter of running enough times into the rain.

Hunched under the mosquito netting, Emma uncapped her pen. In the courtroom ceiling above her translator's hazy head there surely would be a hole. For two thousand years, when it rained anywhere in the world, it had rained over the translator. When it snowed, surely the jury would accuse the translator of hiding behind the snow.

Emma was just about to begin another page when she heard the slap of flip-flops outside her room. You left your sneakers out here, Marcus called through the door.

I know. They were too wet to bring inside.

Well, there are ponds in them now. And some tadpoles swimming around. I could hang them up for you.

Emma opened the door and Marcus raised her sneakers, so waterlogged they hung from his hand like slippers.

I hung mine from the ledge above the toilet, he said, and she moved aside so he could carry her sneakers past her with his liquid ease. Above the commode, he lodged the shoes at a tilt, knotting their soggy laces to the curtain. See? This way they won't fall in the bowl, he said, and, turning around, gestured toward her bed, and she stepped away. He was going to ask her if she wanted to have sex. He was going to offer up the idea as casually as suggesting a game of Boggle.

But he only pointed to her open notebook on the bed. So you write, too, he said.

Oh, no, I don't write. She backed up. I was just, you know, taking notes.

To: eneufeld@pitt.edu
Subject: alive?

Emma, please answer already. I'm sorry
I went off like that in the car but you
didn't even tell me before you bought
your ticket. I can't stop checking my
email and the cats keep meowing for you
at the bathroom door. They think you're
hiding in there, reading.

More notes?

Marcus came up behind her on the balcony the next morning in a pair of orange swim trunks, the waistband so low that she could see where the muscles sloped toward his groin.

Oh, yes, just more boring translator notes. Emma flipped the journal shut. Knocked out of the trees by the wind overnight, dozens of jackfruit now lay splattered on the ground, their insides sugaring the air. Emma wasn't sure if it was their scent or the wet mangy dog on the balcony that was making her sneeze.

I don't know how many more days I can wait out this rain, she said, and blew her nose again.

We should probably go anyway. He handed her the gossip section from yesterday's edition of *O Globo*. Emma immediately recognized the ferry in the photo and the sylphlike sprawl of legs and arms of the man beside her. But what was that look on her face?

Somebody who didn't know better would say it was desire — what a man will deny himself until he can't. Beatriz had written the line at the close of her story "Santiago Martins."

In Portuguese, Beatriz had technically written, what a man will deny himself until he won't.

Emma had thought "can't" made more sense than "won't" for

capturing the boldness and Brazilian spirit of the sentence. As she shivered at her desk in Pittsburgh, the winter creaking in through the windows while Miles snored in the next room, it felt indisputable. Santiago's desire had to be imperative, to carry the weight of fact.

At least in English.

Roberto Rocha stared at the can of olives on his desk. It was the second offering of condiments he'd received from the supermarket across the street. Yet another of his ingratiating novelists had shown up to pitch a manuscript that the young man had read through only once himself. Rocha told him that if he spent as much time revising as he did fantasizing about his books being made into movies, maybe the press would've come close to breaking even at some point in the last seven years.

Such conversations were deadening his senses. He didn't want an offering of canned olives. He wanted someone to show up with a manuscript so unprecedented it made the temperature in his body rise. An author whose sentences were so sublime they made his head ache, who could deliver an image so precise and true he responded with every atom in his body. To keep publishing books that meant nothing to him was turning him into a fraud. A braver man would've given up by now and let the press fold.

Excuse me, Roberto? Flavia stuck her head in the door, her dark glasses low on her nose. Editora Record just called. They want to know if we're going to reissue Beatriz Yagoda's first two books, and said if we're not they'd like to buy the rights to them. They can't get her latest book into the stores fast enough.

Because the poor woman disappeared into a tree?

And that picture of her son.

He is quite the Adonis, isn't he?

Rocha had known that Marcus was going to be exceptional-looking. Beatriz had known it as well, but was too modest to say such a thing about her own child. She spoke with equal modesty about her writing, and never with the air of faux modesty so many of his young writers cultivated now. With Beatriz, modesty wasn't a performance. It was a given, a gracefulness.

Tell Record they can't have the rights, Rocha said. In fact, tell them next Friday we're rereleasing the books ourselves.

Next Friday? Flavia's eyes widened behind her lenses, but Rocha didn't pay attention. He was already considering the best approach to the new cover. He'd need something sleeker but with a deliciousness—an image of cutlery, perhaps, in silver. If he paid Eduardo extra, they could keep the printers going over the weekend and into the evenings. They could hire trucks to deliver the first copies to a few select stores to build excitement. Several years ago, he'd considered reissuing the early novels that Beatriz had published with him but had worried it would make him look desperate—out to remind everyone how relevant he'd once been—and then her last book did so poorly. She wasn't visible anymore, or not until she disappeared.

See if Eduardo can meet this afternoon, Rocha said. No, revise that. Tell him I'll be in his office today at three. We've got to race on this. Once the Comando Vermelho kidnaps their next banker, the media will move on.

There's also this. Flavia held out a small envelope. You said you wanted to see any personal mail as soon as it came in.

Rocha slit open the envelope in one stroke, his fleshy hands

moving with a new ferocity. Folded inside was a room service menu from a hotel in Salvador da Bahia. On the very bottom someone had written a single sentence—If you can't, I
understand—and signed below, S. Martins.

Eduardo at three, please, Rocha said. And Flavia, dear, why
don't you take those olives?

Whether she took them or not, he didn't notice. "Santiago Martins" had affected his sleep. It had been so heartbreakingly Brazilian: a transvestite convinced that the only reason he dressed in
women's clothes was to stay hidden from the police. Beatriz had
attended to the details with her inimitable vividness: Santiago's
dismay at how his back hair caught on the metal zipper of his
dress, the assured way he maneuvered the ladle at his food cart
while filling bowls with shrimp *moqueca* for the better-looking
tourists, his gestures as feminine as those of any of the women vendors in their starched white Baiana dresses along the promenade.

Years after the police had forgotten his crimes, there was Santiago Martins—still ironing his starched white dress at night,
still gossiping in the morning with the other women as they
bought *dendê* oil and dried shrimp and predicted how brutally
the sun would burn by noon.

And one night there was Santiago buying a nightgown for his
mother and Santiago pulling the nightgown over his head in the
privacy of his room. Santiago feeling the satin pour cool as milk
down his back. Desire, Beatriz had written, was what a man will
deny himself until he can't. Rocha had convinced her to change
the verb to "won't." He thought it was subtler, more nuanced.
Beatriz hadn't agreed, but she let him keep the change in. She
knew that he loved the story but felt uneasy about publishing it.
At the time, he'd been the only openly gay editor in Brazil.

Recalling the incident now, he reached for his wallet. How often did one have the chance to rewrite the hesitations of the past? He would reissue the book with Beatriz's original choice and get it out faster than Record ever could. She'd never quite achieved as much bewildering wonder in her later books as she had in the first two she'd published with him. With this reprint, he'd put those early books on the map for good. He'd get them displayed in the front window of every Livraria Cultura in Rio and São Paulo.

First, of course, he'd have to call up the hotel in Salvador listed on the room service menu and pay for S. Martins to stay on another ten days. Once that was arranged, he'd get the new cover done, place the necessary calls to the magazines. He'd remind the country that it was Editora Eco that had launched two of the most startling new works of fiction of the last thirty years. Then, with dignity, with elegance, he'd let whoever still read literature in Rio come by and empty the office of its remaining volumes, and that would be it.

He'd put on his hat and turn off the lights.

Raquel was the only one on the floor when she headed to the elevators. Thiago had gone home to his family hours ago. He'd told her that they could look into the settlement offer from the strikers at the potash mine in the morning. She'd stayed on anyway. As long as she was in the office, she could forget about her missing mother for five, even seven minutes at a time.

On Monday nights, she'd often met her mother at the food-by-the-kilo place around the corner. Over *bolinhos* and marinated asparagus, Raquel would unload her latest grievance about the media and whatever mining incident they were exaggerating now.

Eventually, she'd ask about her mother's day and her mother would talk about her persimmon trees on the balcony, smile timidly, and then bite the tip off one of the asparagus stems on her plate.

Although her mother had given evasive answers like this for years, they still made Raquel feel uneasy and untrusted. To avoid getting angry, she had come to avoid any direct questions about her mother's writing. Chickens laid eggs. Cows and goats produced milk. Every six or seven years her mother produced a book. Of all the unreliable things about her mother, this pattern had remained unchanged. It was as true to her mother's mysterious nature as it was of a palm to produce coconuts.

Even if she never read them, Raquel had appreciated her

mother's books for the sureness of their arrival, for proving that her mother was a functioning person, and despite the reputed darkness people found so alarming in her work, in person her mother was reassuring. All her writer friends thought they stopped by out of admiration for what she wrote, but Raquel was certain that they came more for the attentive way her mother listened to them and their pretentious ideas. Standing now outside the revolving doors of PetroXM, Raquel felt confident that her mother would return eventually and resume her life. She would come back quietly and without any apologies or solutions, but she would come back.

Buoyed by this thought, Raquel hailed a cab to Copacabana. There was no reason she couldn't go to the cheap food-by-the-kilo spot near her mother's anyway, and who knew? Maybe her mother would be sitting at their usual table, waiting for Raquel to find her there. She felt so relieved by this fantasy that she rolled down the window to take in the breeze. She could taste the ocean in it the way it was blowing tonight, rinsing away the stink Thiago liked to call the sweaty ass of Rio.

At the corner before the restaurant, she got out and thought of something she could text him about the strike that really couldn't wait until tomorrow. She was punching in the words on her phone when something yanked at her neck and pulled her off the sidewalk and into a recessed doorway. It was a man's arm, closing around her throat so fast there was no time to cry out. The man already had her crushed against him, her face to the wall, the muzzle of his gun pushing into her back.

You need to tell your brother and that translator to stop screwing around and get the money, you hear me? he said from behind her, breathing into her ear.

She tried to say yes but his arm was still tight around her throat.

I said did you hear me? the man repeated, and then the muzzle of the gun was no longer against her back and she heard a knife snap open, and his other arm appeared, bringing the blade to her neck. Get the money, he said, or one of you is done, *amiga*. They will gun you down. This visit is a favor, eh? You hear what I'm saying?

A few feet away, she heard people strolling by, one of them laughing. If she screamed, they'd surely hear her, but maybe it would increase the chance that he'd panic and slit her throat. Or they wouldn't come for her. Not on a run-down side street in Copacabana, not at ten in the evening.

Then as suddenly as the man had gripped her throat he let go. He was gone. For a moment, Raquel didn't move. She just stood there bracing for something more, something worse. Someone had urinated recently on the slats of cardboard under her feet and the doorway smelled horrible. She hadn't registered the smell until the man let go but didn't know if she should leave yet. What if the man was still lurking nearby, waiting to see where she'd go or who she might call? She pictured her mother dragged into a recessed doorway like this one, full of garbage reeking of urine, imagined how long her mother would have remained there, trembling.

At the thought, Raquel forced herself out onto the sidewalk. A man blurred by on a bicycle and she cried out in alarm. From the jutting hill of a near favela came the stutter of shots of an assault rifle. For a second, the single seam of streetlights running through the favela gleamed brighter. Then the seam folded into the dark.

The whole way to her mother's, Raquel sensed someone waiting for her. He was behind the bus, or pretending to read the headlines at the news kiosk. He was the young man lurching toward her in a blue muscle shirt, or the older one in a cheap suit swearing into his phone

Another block went by and no one jumped her.

Then another.

In five minutes, she would be able to double-lock the doors and eat bowls of cereal in her mother's kitchen. If no one grabbed her before then, if she didn't have a panic attack, she could spend the night in her old room. She'd already passed Belíssima Fashion and the Unibanco. With each building, fewer men looked as though they were waiting to cut her throat. She took in the red stilettos on sale at Lulu's and the window after that, at the bookstore Livraria Cultura—where suddenly there was her mother's face, blown up on a poster wide as a windshield, her unsettling green eyes magnified to the size of headlights.

Next to her mother's face was an equally gigantic image of the cover of her last novel: a sandwich filled with tiny people squirming out the sides like fruitworms. Raquel had told her mother that the cover was too disturbing, that readers wouldn't want to pick it up, and she'd been right. The book had been her mother's least popular in years.

Although now, on the other side of the window, a woman in a Lycra sundress was picking up a copy and a man with a jowly face and mustache was waiting behind her to do the same. As they lifted the books from the stack, Raquel saw her mother's face again, smaller, on the back of each copy and remembered her mother's visit a few weeks ago, the Band-Aid on her neck. How long ago had it been? Her mother had said it was just a cut, that she'd gotten the rooster skin on her old neck caught in a zipper. But maybe it had been the knife of one of Flamenguinho's men. Maybe he'd nicked her as a warning, or it had been the second time he'd pulled her mother off the street and the message had been, This time I will break your skin. From now on, if I let you go, you will be bleeding.

Beatriz was not on the far side of the island either. Emma knew it as soon as the boat nosed up to the dock. There was only one street and nothing along it but stillness and a few tin-roofed buildings. One of them had a sign out front that said it was a restaurant, but it contained only one table, on top of which sat a pair of roosting chickens. As for the prison, a jungled-over path led her and Marcus to a mossy zigzag of crumbling walls. The closest thing they encountered to Beatriz's orchestra of animals was a flock of fanged bats hissing upside down in an archway.

I'm so sorry, Emma said, coming to a stop in the shade of a guava tree to wipe her face. Online it hadn't been clear that all the hotels were on the other side of the island, she said. But still, I shouldn't have dragged you here and caused problems with your sister.

You didn't drag me. Marcus shrugged. I knew it was unlikely we'd find her here, but wherever she is will seem unlikely and Raquel knows the only way to find her is to be a little impulsive.

Marcus twisted one of the guavas off the tree. Thumbing off the skin, he told Emma about a time in high school when his mother stopped cooking or buying food. On one of his trips to the supermarket with his sister, several weeks into the problem, Raquel was yelling about their mother being weak and indulgent then abruptly turned to Marcus and said, Turkey. He went to find it, assuming she was going to try to make their mother's *vatapá*. When they got home, they found their mother in the kitchen grinding peanuts for the sauce, a can of coconut milk already out on the counter.

Neither of us had called to tell her about the turkey, Marcus said. But you must know this about my mother, eh? You have to be patient with her, but also trust your instincts, no?

Emma was about to agree when Marcus abruptly peeled off his sweaty T-shirt. She tried to look politely away. By the time he'd run the shirt up his chest and over the sweat on his back, her effort at restraint had failed completely. The front of her tank top was damp now as well. Even in the shade, the heat was so intense it seemed to be emanating from the stones.

I suppose, she said, this is why they called it the Devil's Cauldron.

Oh, I bet they had far worse names for it than that. Marcus laughed and crouched to examine the blocks of years somebody had etched into one of the stones. This guy must have been a Communist, or maybe a murderer.

At "murderer," they both fell silent. The image of the bulging gun in Flamenguinho's jacket resurfaced in Emma's mind, as he must have intended. And here she was, wasting two days over some passing idea that had made her feel smart on the plane.

When they reached the lone restaurant, Marcus said he was too ravenous to wait and eat on the other side of the island, and Emma felt too embarrassed about the futility of the trip to disagree. Inside, the chickens were clucking around under the table and there was now a tremendous white pig slumbering beside the cash register.

Emma was about to remark that it looked as though nobody was working today and they'd have to wait after all when a small girl emerged from the kitchen swinging a plastic doll by its hair. Marcus asked the girl if she or her companion might know something about lunch.

The girl said her mother had a fish stew going on the stove and Marcus said marvelous, they'd take two bowls. Given the hygiene standards of the establishment, Emma was about to say a second bowl wouldn't be necessary when the girl abruptly spun around and disappeared back into the kitchen. Marcus, still shirtless, said he was going to check in with the boatman at the dock waiting to take them back to the other side. Left alone at the wobbly table, Emma tried not to think about how ravenous she had become. One of the chickens pecked at her sandal and she kicked it away and felt ashamed.

She wished she'd brought along something with words on it, even an old magazine from the hotel. Besides her water and sunscreen, all she had in her bag was her notebook.

So she opened it.

In: *Preposition.* Used to indicate inclusion in a physical space or within something abstract or immaterial: *in a panic,* for example, or *in a fantasy taking place while sitting between a sleeping pig and a pair of chickens, one of which has just relieved itself on the floor.*

The fish *moqueca*. Emma felt it rising in her throat as soon as the ferry began to move. In one heave at the railing, she returned the fish to the sea.

Ai, Emma! Marcus grabbed her arm so she wouldn't tip over the railing. You should drink some water. Come. He began to lead her toward the stairs up to the snack bar but Emma felt too queasy to climb them.

I'll wait here, she said, flopping on a pile of emergency rafts. On the way to the island, she hadn't noticed how often the ferry rocked beneath them, but she felt it now, every tiny rise and fall. It was possible, she recognized in her nauseous state, that she had nothing at all to offer in the search for her author. To avoid further embarrassment, she needed to book a flight home tomorrow. She'd call Miles and apologize for letting his emails go unanswered. They'd lived together this long, knew which mug the other preferred for coffee and which for tea. There was no reason she could not go with him to speak to caterers and commit to a wedding date.

Horizontal on the emergency rafts, her eyes closed, she was nearly convinced. She could be grateful for Miles and his steadiness. They would delight in exercise and recycling.

Then Marcus returned, leaning over her with a bottle of water still wet from where it had been submerged in ice. He asked if he should leave her to rest there a little longer and she knew that the appropriate answer was yes. But to reach his wrist was a matter of inches and there were her fingers, already trickling up his arm. To kiss her author's son just once, atop a pile of emergency rafts, didn't have to mean anything.

Unless she did it again.

And then again in the last row of the bus back to Rio.

And in the taxi from the bus terminal, in the brief darkness of the tunnel into Copacabana.

This will have to stop, she said.

As for Marcus, he left his hand where it was, between her legs.

Between: *Preposition.* **1.** By the common action of <*between the two of them*> but also used to designate a difference, a setting apart <*between an author and her son*>. **2.** Used to indicate an interval <*between a brief tunnel in Rio and the distant Pittsburgh of one's cats*>.

At 4 a.m., Raquel stopped reading. She was two hundred pages into what was, or was not, the novel her mother had been working on when she staged her vanishing into the tree. Until this evening, Raquel had only gone into her mother's poker accounts on the computer. She'd left the Word documents closed, but that had been before she'd been dragged, gagging, into a doorway. She was so tired that she had to read each sentence three times but knew she wouldn't be able to sleep until she got to the end of it. The novel was set in the seventies, the pages alternating between the same two scenes again and again. In each telling, the scenes devolved into long stretches of random numbers and letters as if her mother had lost control of her hands, the pages filling with 3r#T)_4tg09NGJOP!@#)%$*PGM:-t-gtkltpjhhjIasd920-4tiu34-tu3y5 -2y-u9jgdfpgj, and on and on.

It was the work of a broken person, somebody too bewildered by her own thoughts to punch in anything but nonsense. Both scenes were about a woman who'd graduated from a university in Rio in the early seventies, as Raquel's mother had. The first scene took place at Cine Paissandu, the movie house where artsy types had brooded and commiserated during the dictatorship. In every version of the scene, something went wrong with the film: the reel broke or the sound system started to garble. While the audience waited for things to resume, the woman stepped into the alley behind the theater for a cigarette. The other smokers headed back inside, but she was too restless to join them. She sat down on the step for another cigarette in the alley, assuming she was alone.

But she wasn't. There was a shadow. It drew closer and—

The sentence stopped, unfinished. After a page break, the same scene began again with the same woman alone in the same alley. Sometimes it took seven pages to get to the shadow, sometimes just a paragraph, but every time the shadow was about to reach the woman, her mother's words came to an end.

In each version of the scene, things began identically, except the woman stepped into the alley wearing a blue linen dress instead of a cotton one. Or she was wearing a skirt. Or she'd placed her cigarette in her left hand instead of her right. As if it was only a matter of getting the right attire or placement of the cigarette to alter what happened next.

But the shadow kept approaching anyway, and the painfully precise descriptions of the woman's clothing would continue, down to the square shape of the metal buttons on her blouse and the name of the maid who had pressed the shirt for her that morning, and then the shadow closed in, clamping his hand over her mouth, and the passage broke off again, unfinished.

The next page would be either another version or a different scene completely, set in Salvador da Bahia with what seemed like the same woman but married with a baby and on holiday. The three of them were sitting at a busy restaurant by the ocean. In every version of the second scene, the father banged his hand on the table and told the woman to stop gazing off. He ridiculed her for choosing a restaurant with such small portions and poor service—the sort of comments Raquel's father had made in restaurants.

Or the man Raquel had assumed was her father. Especially after he died, people had remarked on how little she looked like him. Of course, they'd said the same about her mother. So who is it you look like? her friends' parents always asked after seeing her next to her mother and Marcus. She'd always found it curious that her mother had married her father so quickly after meeting him and had taken his last name. Maybe it was to erase any doubts about his paternity.

Or maybe this half-finished story was fiction and only the details bore a resemblance to their family. For all Raquel knew, her mother's drafts always broke off this way at difficult moments until her mother figured out what she wanted to do next. In the restaurant scene, just when it seemed as though the woman and her husband were about to have it out with each other, the woman would flee into some surreal description of the fish on her plate winking up at her with its oily eye, or of the man seated at the next table reading a yellowed newspaper from seventy-three years ago. Or her mother would simply write CHECK ON THIS, as if the date of the newspaper or the kind of fish staring up at the woman from her plate mattered tremendously.

Raquel rubbed at her temples. She'd always known if she read her mother's fiction it would be devastating or alienating or both. What she needed was to lie down and take a break. The further in she read, the more the scenes devolved into frustrating trails of random letters: two words and then AOGFH$#T)IGR...and then a description of a waiter's shoes and then ^OIEWQJGFLD GASDFJHEWR#$TIGJG)GJGTJBHT)TH)L:O))#$*()U_)ORGN GWE@#)R*...and on and on, filling the pages where the rest of the novel should have been.

Raquel wondered which of her mother's friends would know if the story about the shadow and the alley was true. Maybe none of them would know, or maybe her mother had confided in some unreliable writer friend during one of her slumps, and that friend had told all the others. Maybe the disdain Raquel had sensed that her mother's friends felt about her lack of interest in literature wasn't disdain at all, but unease with what they knew about her and she didn't. Maybe it was pity—a possibility that made her despise them even more.

But this mess of unfinished sentences on her mother's computer wasn't a book for other readers, or it wasn't yet. If the scene in the alley was true, it belonged to her as much as it did to her mother. And to no one else.

Rocha pulled out his most trusted saucepan and a bottle of his favorite Chilean Carmenere, the unparalleled Veramonte, which he'd chilled overnight. Out past the kitchen, Alessandro had turned up the Salieri aria playing on their gramophone, *Prima la musica, poi le parole,* and had stretched out on the couch with the newspaper.

Ave Maria, Alessandro said. Did you see this? He held up the cover of the gossip section for Rocha to read. It was another photo of Beatriz's son and her American translator on the Ilha Grande ferry, only this time the young woman appeared to be vomiting over the railing.

Ai, que vulgar. Rocha took the page from Alessandro to study it more closely. It was the third paper this week with a feature on Beatriz and her continuing absence. He'd always thought there was nothing better for a writer's reputation than dying. But even more promising than dying, it seemed, was to magnificently disappear.

Which gave him an idea.

The idea, at least in the elevator, was to have sex just once before letting Raquel know they were back in Rio. Only once, Emma said twice, just to get it out of our systems. Then we can really focus on finding your mother without distracting each other. Sex just once in his mother's sweltering apartment and that would be it.

When they opened the door, however, the apartment wasn't sweltering at all. It was cool, the air-conditioning humming in every room, though Emma was certain she had turned it off before leaving for Ilha Grande.

Raquel must have come by and forgotten to turn it off, Marcus said. Come here. He pulled at her hips until she tilted toward him. If they'd been standing anywhere but in front of her author's bookshelves, the titles she'd run her fingers over for years like sacred scrolls, Emma was sure she would have had more restraint, would not be lifting her own dress this way over her head.

When Marcus slid her polka-dot underwear down over her knees, she murmured something about thinking about this a little more. But she didn't want to think. She wanted to fling her underwear down the hall with her toe.

So she did, and the motion was divine.

Now there was nothing in the way.

On the balcony, Raquel was well into her third bowl of Sucril-hos. There hadn't been anything else that had appealed to her in her mother's fridge, and nothing that could satisfy like bingeing on a box of frosted flakes.

And so it was with a constellation of soggy Sucrilhos floating across the milk in her bowl that she stepped back into the apartment and heard panting. A distinct knocking coming from the hallway as the rhythm got faster, the panting more pronounced. Raquel clenched her spoon as she raged into the living room, milk swishing over the lip of her bowl.

Meu Deus, Marcus! she shouted, and began to sob. Someone had just pressed a knife to her neck. It was possible her father was a hideous stranger in an alley. And now here was her brother, thrusting himself into their mother's translator, knocking their mother's beloved books to the floor.

We're all going to be killed, you idiots. Don't you get it?

His eyes wide, Marcus extracted himself from Emma and turned, leaving Raquel to stare at her brother fully erect in a tex-tured condom the purplish pink of bubble gum.

Caralho, Marcus, she said, put your *pau* away. Beside him, Emma was already yanking her dress over her head so franti-cally that she knocked down several large books that had been sitting on top of the shelf behind her. As they crashed to the floor, an envelope fluttered out and slid across the hallway, disappearing under the opposite shelf. Any other week, Raquel would have dismissed the envelope as more of her mother's endless clutter and left it there.

But everything was filled with portent now, could be the distance between seeing her mother again and not.

Move the shelf, Marcus, hurry up, she ordered. What are you waiting for?

Bare as he'd arrived twenty-nine years ago at Hospital Geral de Bonsucesso, Marcus tugged and pulled at the shelf, but the books were tightly packed and shelved three deep. Even with Raquel's help, it was too heavy to budge.

Emma got on her knees and began pulling out handfuls of books to lighten the shelf. Raquel had never felt less inclined to join forces with her mother's translator, but she did it, making a point of pulling out the books faster and harder, knocking Emma's stacks out of her way.

When they'd finally extracted enough books to move the shelf, Raquel made sure she was the one who got to the letter first. It was postmarked a year ago and from Rio. She couldn't think of who in the same city would bother to send her mother a letter until she pulled out the engraved card inside. Of course. It was from her mother's pretentious first editor, Roberto. The card contained nothing but fussy details about a dinner party and what would be served.

It's nothing, Raquel said. Just a frivolous card from a friend about a party. She tossed it in the tin trash can by the TV. She knew that Emma was going to retrieve it but wouldn't dare reach into the garbage until Raquel had left the room. How could she, with her polka-dot underwear hanging from the handle of an umbrella by the door?

Raquel crossed her arms and stared out at the persimmon trees on the balcony. She couldn't make Emma leave. But she could make her wait.

To: eneufeld@pitt.edu
Subject: Re: alive?

Emma, vanishing like this is crazy. Your
parents said they haven't heard from you
either. Julia from your department has
left a hundred messages on the landline
saying you need to confirm your office
hours ASAP for the spring semester. I'm
sorry I flipped out on the way to the
airport but what you're doing now is
cruel. You need to answer. I'm sure
everyone in Beatriz's family is grateful
you're there and you've been a tremendous
help. Just tell me where you are.

Hidden in the guest room, Emma enjoyed her findings quietly. It had been excruciating to wait for Raquel to leave the room but it had been worth it. She was so jittery from reading Rocha's card that she'd stopped trying to hear what Raquel was telling Marcus in the kitchen. It was too hard to make out what they were saying from two rooms away. All she could gather was that Raquel was going to leave in the morning and Marcus wanted to go as well, but Raquel kept saying no, that he had become too much of a liability after getting his picture in all the gossip columns. Neither of them had mentioned Emma's appearance in the photos as well, which was a relief, though also insulting and dismissive—a conflict of emotions that was standard fare for a translator. Emma had come to find the unease this conflict produced in her curiously alluring. She couldn't help winding herself tighter and tighter around it like a thread around a spool.

At one point, she thought she heard Marcus suggest that if they were going to pursue something based on their mother's writing, they had to admit that Emma knew much more about their mother as a writer than they did.

Or perhaps that was just what Emma wanted to overhear.

In any case, she had her triumph in this card on her lap, elegantly written in the formidable script of Roberto Rocha. She hadn't known that Beatriz had stayed in touch with him after moving on to her trade publisher in Portugal. The card was mostly gossip and exhaustive descriptions of entrées. But in one of the paragraphs, after an elaborate report on a lemongrass sauce for chicken kebabs, Rocha wrote, All of this is to say we'll be having chicken when you come next week, my dear. As for your phone call, you know I'm always here to serve as your Gonzaga.

Emma knew of only one Gonzaga in Brazilian literature. To confirm her hunch, she clicked out of her email, away from Miles and the urgent requests from Julia for her office hours. The information floated up from the turbid sea of Google trivia: twenty-six hits for Antonio Gonzaga, youngest son of the Gonzaga mining empire in the state of Minas Gerais, benefactor of various *modernismo* writers and the cubist painter Vera Coutinho.

She typed in Roberto Rocha next, something quickening inside her. Before she could find the website for Rocha's press, she had to scroll through pages of lifestyle articles about various extravagant Rocha siblings—one who'd bought a $50,000 Italian wedding gown and one who traveled only by helicopter and threw wild parties on his three-story yacht. After all the glitz of his brothers and sisters, the website for Rocha's press seemed not just outdated but primitive. It featured nothing but a list of titles. There were no pictures of the authors, no links or blurbs. The only image on the page was a picture of the ornate colonial building on Rua Francisco Sá that housed the press, a photograph that seemed to say, We are above websites and embedded links. Look at what we own.

If Beatriz had asked Rocha to be her Gonzaga before, it was hard to imagine she wouldn't go to him for money now. Raquel had said that all her mother's accounts were overdrawn. What-ever cash Beatriz had taken with her into that almond tree was going to run out. That is, if she hadn't sought out her Gonzaga already.

Emma got up from the bed to share her idea with Marcus and Raquel but stopped at the door. It would be better to tell Marcus later, alone. Or even better just to go and say nothing in case she was completely wrong again. She didn't want to lead them astray a second time or repeat that humiliation. She could just stick to her story of leaving in the morning for Pittsburgh, which she couldn't follow through on now, not after this card from Rocha. For a second, she forced her mind back to Shadyside, to her drafty bedroom, Miles grinding his teeth beside her in the dark, the radiator banging in the basement as if someone were trapped and thrashing inside it with a giant stack of pots. No, she couldn't go, not yet.

Sitting back down on one of the twin beds in the guest room, she opened her journal to a new page. CHAPTER TWO: **JACKPOT.**

Jackpot: Americanism; of uncertain origin. **1.** A substantial win following a gamble. **2.** A sudden influx of fortune that may lead a person to reconsider how much she is willing to risk next, as in: *After a poor choice or two, the American translator, like others in her country, has been known to go to extraordinary lengths to prove she, too, can hit the jackpot.* **See also:** stubborn. **3.** A word used to justify risking more in pursuit of something unlikely. **See also:** redemption.

Editora Eco was a landfill of manuscripts. Emma had never seen so many stacks of yellowed, languishing pages in a single place. Maybe Rocha was trying to scare new writers away. On top of one of the stacks someone had left a rather sad looking can of olives.

Can I help you? the receptionist asked from behind a pillar of books and manuscripts beside her desk.

Bom dia, Emma said. Is Roberto Rocha in today?

He just left for Salvador. What was it you needed?

I came to ask him about... Emma paused, having just noticed the book lying next to the receptionist's phone. Is that a Beatriz Yagoda novel?

Yes, we're rereleasing *Have You Tasted the Butterflies.* Isn't it gorgeous? The girl handed the book to Emma. The new cover was sleek and minimal, with nothing on it but a silver fork and matching slender spoon. It looked like an image of a remodeled kitchen in *Architectural Digest* and couldn't have been more at odds with the lush chaos of leafy plants on the original cover from the seventies. Over the two years it had taken Emma to translate the book, she'd come to know those plants as intimately as the pores on her nose.

Everybody's rushing to reissue her books now that she's

disappeared, the girl said, and then leaned forward, as if she'd just heard a curious sound under the floor. You were in the pictures on the ferry with her son, in the newspaper. You're her translator, the American.

Those pictures were very misleading, Emma replied. I assure you, she said. But her *te juro* came out more like *joelho,* the word for knee.

They were all fading now on the balcony—her mother's beloved persimmon trees. Raquel had tried more water and then less but it didn't seem to matter. Whatever she had given or withheld, the four fruits whose skin had been ripening to a deep orange in her mother's care had now wilted to a rotting brown.

Whether they were dying or not, she'd made Marcus promise to keep tending them after she left this morning for Salvador. If they gave up this fast on her mother's trees, what was next? What if their mother suddenly came home and found them out there, abandoned?

You need to piss on them, Thiago had told her yesterday at work. He said his grandfather swore by a little female urine for a failing tree. Something about the hormones in a woman's pee, especially right after she woke up. You should sleep there and piss all over them first thing in the morning, he'd advised her, and though she had yet to squat over the persimmons, his counsel had been helpful, as she'd realized she was not as upset or determined to save them as she had thought.

She'd at least solved the problem of Emma before heading to Salvador. As Emma was finally going back to Pittsburgh today, Raquel hadn't told her about her flight this morning. She didn't want to risk that Emma might stick around. She was certain that her hunch wasn't like Emma's. Her mother had been writing about Salvador just before she vanished and hadn't finished. Even Thiago had agreed that she should go. It's an awful time for you to be out, he had said, but you need to go and find your old lady. Tell her to get back in her tree, where she belongs.

With Thiago's blessing, Raquel had felt fairly at ease until she reached the airport. At her terminal, she started to feel someone watching her. Or she was getting paranoid. To calm herself, she bought two ham-and-cheese *salgados,* but they only made her thirsty and bloated. In the Thursday paper there'd been a picture of three women piled like chicken parts in a shopping cart, their limbs so brutally mutilated it was hard to tell where one body ended and another began. It was entirely possible that one of Flamenguinho's men was here now, would stalk her in Salvador until she found her mother and then slaughter them both.

On the news, when they reported the deaths, all they'd say was that she was Beatriz Yagoda's daughter. They'd flash an image of her round, ordinary face for a second, maybe two, before going back to her green-eyed, high-cheekboned mother receiving the Jabuti Prize at twenty-nine on TV. And that would be it, her life over. Thiago would go home to his wife and his children and hire someone younger to replace her.

Raquel squeezed her head between her palms, unsure of what to do, wondering if she should just go back home. But to what? She'd already taken the days off work and spent four hundred *reais* on her ticket. It was too late to get back her deposit on the hotel. Balancing the expense against her fear, she boarded the plane. Ahead of her in line was a tall bald man with a thick keloid scar across the back of his neck. A knife scar.

Or just a scar from a fall from a horse. Or out of a car. She ran a hand over her hot face. Her mouth felt so dry it was an effort to swallow. She was going to have to find some way to stop this paranoia. All day long she dealt with union leaders shouting at her. They got right up in her face, threatening to coerce every miner in Brazil to walk out on PetroXM, and she stared them down. She wasn't going to fall apart now. She just had to focus on the aisles one at a time, on the chubby little girl who had just peered over the top of a seat and then disappeared. Raquel forced herself to concentrate on that seat, on seeing the round face of that girl again. But when she got closer, there was no child in the row. Only a middle-aged woman picking at her cuticles and reading *Have You Tasted the Butterflies* by Beatriz Yagoda.

Have You Tasted the Butterflies by the still-missing Beatriz Yagoda joins her other titles on the best-seller list this week—and here is some other wild news for you Yagoda fans. Radio Globo has just received a report that a second writer has taken refuge in the trees of Rio. A young novelist named Vicente Tourinho was last seen scaling a banyan tree in the lovely Jardim de Alá.

What's going on with our writers, Brazil? What's sending them into our city parks and up into the trees?

Emma hid behind a pillar in the baggage claim. In the past, the sight of her green valise coming toward her amid the dark heaps of luggage had always brought her pleasure. But then she'd never attempted to hide from anyone arriving on the same flight.

Maybe she'd get lucky and Raquel's luggage would emerge first.

But no, there was her green valise now, spitting out from behind the rubber flaps and moving around the carousel toward Raquel, who was staring at it as if she'd just discovered a thick hair growing back on her chin.

When Raquel reached down and yanked the valise off the carousel, Emma decided she had no choice but to step out sheepishly from behind the post. Before she left, she'd told Marcus where she was headed but asked him not to tell Raquel, not until she had something to report to redeem herself. The night before, she'd made a point of putting her things by the door to make it clear that she was leaving in the morning. And she had left for the airport. If she'd lied about her destination, it was to avoid irritating Raquel further. *Traduttore, tradittore* — that tired, tortured Italian cliché.

If only she'd been born a man in Babylon when translators had been celebrated as the makers of new language. Or during the Renaissance, when translation was briefly seen as a pursuit as visionary as writing. She would have been in her element then. During the Renaissance, no translator had to apologize for following her instincts to champion the work of one of the most extraordinary, under-recognized writers of her time.

The seconds it took to reach Raquel felt like each one had a century folded inside it. Look, Emma said, coming to a stop in front of her. This isn't what it seems. I know it looks like I followed you here, but honestly—

You said you were going to finally leave us alone. You said you were going to Pittsburgh. Raquel's voice was getting shriller with each word.

I won't be here long, I swear. I'll just find Rocha and—

Rocha? What's he doing here?

He came to Salvador yesterday, Emma said. Isn't that why you're here?

I don't have to tell you why I'm here.

No, of course not. Emma reached for her green valise but Raquel stuck out her foot to stop the wheels.

Where's Rocha staying?

I don't know, Emma said. When I find him, I'll call you.

Oh, you will. Raquel crossed her arms. And what are you going to do for my mother if you find her? Are you going to pay off her debt? Are you going to protect her from the loan shark you thought was her friend?

I . . . Well, I was thinking I might . . .

You have no idea. Raquel snorted. Admit it, and you should keep in mind that they'll kill you same as they would me and Marcus. They won't care that you're American.

I'm aware of that possibility, Emma said, though in truth she was aware of it only the way a person might hear a faint rumble of thunder on a dry day and find its menacing sound exciting without believing there was any real reason to go inside. If you need me for anything, she offered Raquel, I gave the number of my hotel to your brother.

And with that, she wheeled her bright valise toward the exit and the midday sun waiting outside. By noon, Beatriz had written in her first novel, the heat in Brazil was an animal's mouth. It would swallow anything to feed itself.

To: eneufeld@pitt.edu
Subject: Re: Re: alive?

Emma, you have to stop this. Are you
still upset about what my mother said? I
should have defended you, I recognize
that, but honestly, I thought it would be
easier to just move on and talk about
something else. My mother had her first
kid at twenty. She doesn't understand. I
won't let her drive you crazy over the
wedding plans, I promise. We don't even
have to do the wedding. We can elope or
wait, whatever. Just call, Emma. These
people in Brazil are not your life.

Emma checked the bolt on the lock. The showerhead in the bathroom was loose, which had increased her anxiety about the door. In her panic, she'd called Marcus and then finally written to Miles with the name of her hotel in case she disappeared.

The lock on her door felt solid enough, however, and besides the faulty showerhead, the room was fine. The carpet had no stains and there was a welcoming wooden desk in the corner. Wide and sturdy, it was the sort of place where a person might sit and get her thoughts to stop spewing like hot rocks out of a volcano. Emma pulled out the chair and sat down. At first, all she could do was stare at the wall and feel futile, but that was something. Wasn't the despair of feeling useless central to the modern human condition? Wasn't that what *Don Quijote* was all about?

To shore up what sense of self-regard she had left, she opened her notebook. Perhaps it was time for her alter-haze to speak on the stand.

Emma collapsed on the first bench in the shade. She'd thought it wouldn't take more than a morning or two to find where Rocha was lodging, but she'd already gone into fifteen five-star establishments and on every block there were more. Once again, she'd overestimated her grasp of Brazil. Sunburned and hungry, she felt a wave of dizziness and lowered her head between her knees.

Under the shade of the same banyan tree, a Bahian woman with a deep purple feather in her head wrap was selling fried, steaming mounds of *acarajé*. Emma could smell the *dendê* oil, the onions and yucca stewing in the sauce. Some lunch, senhora? the woman asked without looking up.

Please, Emma said, eyeing the woman's feather again. It was the black-purple of wet beets, of rubies gleaming in the back of a drawer.

Is that feather from a shop nearby, by any chance? Emma asked.

Eh, the woman said. See the hat man behind the Aram Yamí Hotel, over on Santo Antônio Street.

Emma repeated the name of the hotel and the woman nodded, handing her a plastic-based napkin to accompany her *acarajé*. Emma took a bite and her eyes bulged at the sudden blaze in her mouth. Everything had an infernal aspect in Salvador. The hot pepper, the heat. Her mouth in flames, she unfolded her map to see where she was. She hadn't come here to go wandering after feathers.

Unless she had.

In any case, there was Santo Antônio, a mere two blocks away.

The hat man gestured for her to step closer. They were alone in the dim store and Emma wasn't sure she wanted to get any closer. In his stained undershirt, the hat man was holding out to her what he said were the rare purple feathers of a macaw, but they weren't really purple at all. They were blood-colored.

Maybe you prefer the feathers of the jabiru, he said. Do you have a particular hat in mind?

No, not yet, Emma admitted, and he motioned to the forest of hat stands crowding the back of the store. There was a whole stand of the white fedoras that samba musicians wore, another of the jaunty banana-shaped hats for *forró*. But also a rack of floppy cotton sun visors and stiff, colorful straw hats with wide, flamboyant rims. Emma didn't know if she had enough charisma to pull off any of them, but this trip she hadn't been able to avoid the sun as she had in the past. On other trips, she'd carefully orchestrated her days so she could be inside or in the shade by midday for fear that she'd burn. And she'd been right. Out in the hottest hours now, she could feel on her face and arms how irreparably she was burning.

From the nearest stand, she picked up a cream-colored hat with a wide brim and put it on. Miles would have found it a ridiculous choice, destined to end up crumpled at the back of their closet with her other impulse buys from Brazil. Behind her, she heard the hat man shuffling closer. She turned to him.

May I? He slipped a thin dark feather into the band. I don't get martins that often, he said. They only winter here.

Emma stepped in front of the grimy mirror on the far wall. The feather was not the one the woman at the *acarajé* stand had been wearing. This one was longer and had a steely bluish sheen. Between the dark feather and the giant white brim of the hat, she looked like a woman who was slightly off her rocker, or maybe just a woman with a sense of humor, who wasn't willing to wait for some impossible alignment of the stars to enjoy her life.

I can pull out some other feathers for you to try. The hat man eyed her, making it clear that he would be happy to pull out a few other things for her as well. But she said the martin was purple enough.

After settling the bill, she gave a little tilt to the brim and, restored, found her way across the hot street into the lobby of the Aram Yamí Hotel.

The Aram Yamí suited Roberto Rocha impeccably. Upscale and colonial, it was the sort of hotel in which Alessandro would have gone on about his grandmothers scrubbing the floors of such a place for Rocha's grandmothers.

But Alessandro was not here. And in his absence, Rocha had no problem indulging his love of rosewood tables with cabriole legs and the heavy giltwood mirrors in the halls. The voluptuousness of it all enchanted him. Every old object could be a correlative to an injustice if one wanted to see the world that way. But what for? A meticulously carved mahogany settee was still a marvelous settee. Its elegance didn't have to be tainted by the thought of his grandmother's staff on their knees, rubbing in the oil to preserve the gleam of the wood.

Rocha had despised his grandmother, always tinkling her silver service bells and telling him what an odd boy he was, how he had something in his voice that made people nervous.

His loafers removed, Rocha lowered himself onto the bed. It creaked under his weight. Down the hall, a group of American tourists had begun to natter outside the elevator, making it impossible to take a proper rest. Soon, thankfully, the elevator ferried them away and he was almost asleep when the room phone rang.

I'm sorry to disturb you, Senhor Roberto, the receptionist said, but we have a woman in the lobby here to see you.

Is that so? Well, tell her I'll be right down.

He slid his loafers on again, lifted his bifocals from the bed-side table. It was so like Beatriz to be the one to find him. And on the very day he arrived. Surely he'd be able to shake some-thing out of her—a novella or a handful of new stories. She knew he would respect her privacy, wouldn't give away her whereabouts to anyone.

Bing.

The elevator doors parted and Roberto Rocha summoned his most confident, admiring smile. Where was she? The only woman he spotted in the quiet lobby was a gangly tourist wear-ing a giant cream-colored hat that gave her something of the air of a flapper. When the woman with the hat got up and started to move in his direction, he thought it must be a coincidence.

Boa tarde, the woman said. I'm Beatriz's American translator.

He made the face he reserved for vinegar. Was it you who just called? Did you just ask reception to ring my room and rouse me from my nap?

I'm terribly sorry, she said. I can come back later. I was just hoping I could speak to you for a few minutes about Beatriz.

Is her son here with you as well?

Marcus? Oh, no, I came alone. The translator blushed under her broad hat. Her Portuguese wasn't terrible for an American, but she was a nervous girl and too tall. She made him feel absurd, lifting his face to her like a schoolboy, exposing all the rolls of flesh under his chin.

He took a step back to regain control of the conversation. I presume you've spoken with Beatriz.

Well, no . . . I — well, are you here to meet with her?

Of course, Rocha said.

So she's definitely here, in Bahia.

I'm afraid I'm not at liberty to disclose her location, he said.

Well, perhaps you could relay a message. The translator stepped closer, towering over him again. It's about her safety. If she wants to leave Brazil, I want her to know I can help her. She could get a residency in Iowa at the International Writing Program there, or I could get her a longer-term teaching job with —

Because teaching at an American university, he interrupted, is the pot of gold at the end of every writer's rainbow?

I just want to help her get out of danger.

And into the sanctuary of one of your just American institutions.

Senhor Roberto, all I want to do is help.

Oh, I have no doubt, he said. All Americans ever want to do is help. If you'll excuse me, I'm really quite tired. He gave the translator a nod as he turned away and felt her blanch behind him. For months, Alessandro had been warning him that he was turning into a dried-up lemon of a man. It wouldn't have killed him to admit that he had no idea where to find Beatriz either, that the day before he'd arrived she'd vanished from the hotel where she'd registered as S. Martins, having persuaded the hotel to give her cash for the remaining nights he'd paid for her to stay there. He'd been furious at such a blatant manipulation of his generosity, and furious at her for making him travel all this way for nothing.

Although that didn't give him a reason to be rude to her translator, whose name he'd already forgotten.

Beatriz had written a curious story once about five brothers who had trouble remembering names, even each other's. At dinner, to get one another's attention, they'd throw bits of bread crust or sausage across the table. As grown men, they had trouble staying in love. They'd turn to touch the women beside them in bed and realize they had no memory of what their names were. In middle age, they struggled to recall their own names and had to call their parents for a reminder. However, by then their parents were hard of hearing and couldn't differentiate among their sons' voices on the phone. Whoever called, they would reply, Bruno—your name is Bruno, sweetheart. Their sons would then murmur the name to themselves as they buttoned their coats, trying to hold on to it until they got out the door. When they saw one another on the street, they'd shout, It's me—Bruno! But *I'm* Bruno, the other would answer. Mother just told me. And the two brothers would stare at each other with—what had Beatriz called it?—the terrifying conviction of lost men.

The first time Rocha read the story, the terrifying conviction of those brothers reckoning with one another in the street stopped him cold. He'd been sitting in his office, and for a minute everything on his desk had an unsettling glimmer, like the scales on a just-killed fish or the glint of tinfoil floating on dark water in a well.

To: eneufeld@pitt.edu
Subject: in the next five days

Senhora Neufeld,

If I don't get my money this week, I'll be
kidnapping your friend Marcus and taking
one of his ears as interest.

Why? Because it's due. You're taking too
long. I treat all my debtors the same. I
believe in equality. If someone doesn't
pay what they owe me, I go to their
family. Unless, of course, there is an
American with nice legs involved and
what's owed to me is on its way.

Um beijo do
Flamenguinho

Emma read the email with her computer facing the window and then facing away from it. She had thought it might keep Beatriz safe a little longer, her sin of omission at the hotel bar about how much money a new novel by Beatriz would generate in English. But perhaps that had been a mistake. If she hadn't played along with Flamenguinho's assumptions, maybe he wouldn't have thought to start wagering with Marcus.

She felt a longing for her parents, for their reassurance, for the effortlessness of a conversation in her own language. If she called her parents now, though, they would just plead for her to come home. They would stop sleeping. They would send Miles to fetch her and contact the U.S. Embassy, which would lead to the Brazilian police, and Raquel would be furious. She was adamant that they were too corrupt to be of any help and would just sell the story about her mother's gambling to the media.

But maybe Raquel would see things differently now, with this threat to Marcus.

Absolutely not. No police, Raquel said when Emma called and read her the email. They'll make everything worse. Print out the email. Let's meet at a café, and don't cry or look scared when you leave your room, Raquel warned her. You need to look composed. In control.

Emma nodded, though she had no idea how she might compose herself until she remembered her new hat. She set it on her head, tilting the wide brim at a lighthearted angle, though she was shaking. By the time she reached the lobby, she was so terrified she had to sit down. She pulled out her notebook to steady herself with a little fantasy, to disappear for just a moment into the relief of make-believe — into the plea hidden in every fiction for immortality.

Raquel didn't know what to make of Emma's enormous new hat. They'd just sat down for coffee and, staring across at the odd dark feather in it, she wondered if her mother's translator was losing her mind. Otherwise, why start wearing a giant hat now and make it even easier for someone to stalk her through Salvador?

Raquel had brought the pages she'd found on her mother's computer, thinking that Emma might discover something in them that she couldn't. But at the sight of that hat on Emma's head, with its baffling inky-blue feather, Raquel now saw the idea as desperate and absurd. Emma was as susceptible to suppressing common sense as her mother was.

I think Rocha will do it, Emma was saying now. He'll definitely loan the money. Why wouldn't he?

Because he's a snob, Raquel said. And online gambling isn't an aristocratic pursuit. She shoved one of the chocolate *brigadeiros* she'd ordered into her mouth. Rocha probably just sent the money that one time because it was nothing to him. He was probably embarrassed for her.

Raquel looked away from the table, mortified at what she'd admitted, and to Emma, of all people. She had a vivid memory of Rocha coming by the apartment when her mother was in one of her slumps. Before he arrived, Raquel had picked up all the clothes from the floor and guided her mother into the shower and combed her hair. It had been like preparing a giant, glass-eyed doll. She'd yelled at her mother afterward. It had been such a relief to be angry at her again, for her mother to be recovered enough that Raquel could furiously demand an apology.

With all the bank statements and their hundreds of subtraction signs, she'd fantasized about pushing her mother's face into the debt the way people did with their dogs, and saying to her, Look what you've done this time. Look.

Yet here, in Salvador, Raquel's capacity for anger seemed to be depleted. She couldn't cry in front of her mother's translator. If she did, Emma would take over everything.

You printed out the email, right? Can I see it, please?

Emma passed it across the table and asked Raquel if she'd read the news about the writer who'd disappeared into a tree in the Jardim de Alá.

I know the girl he raped, Raquel said. She's the daughter of a congressman. Of all the asshole writers to follow my mother's lead.

But no one will see it that way. Emma shook her head, making her ridiculous feather quiver in her hat. Tourinho's not in your mother's league. His work is derivative and predictable. He's exactly the kind of writer who would climb into a tree to imitate someone who is the real thing. The real thing, Raquel, Emma repeated, her eyes gleaming, as if that were all this was about: whose words dazzled more.

Emma, Raquel said slowly, you do realize there is a very good chance you could die here, and wearing a giant hat like that only makes it easier for someone to follow you. They'll cut off your ears and send them to me or to your husband and think nothing of it.

Emma lowered her eyes. Please stop saying that. I'm not married. I was living with a boyfriend, but I'm here now and I'm not going to leave until we find your mother.

Raquel pinched open the clasp on her purse. I'll show you something, she said, but you have to promise not to do anything with it without my permission.

Permission: From the Latin for *yielding.* **1.** Formal consent, as in: *A translator must acquire permission to publish a story consisting of words that are not her own but that also incidentally are.* **See also:** paradox. **2.** Authorization, as in: *If an author vanishes, her translator must receive written permission from the executor of the author's estate or her nearest of kin.* **3.** The act of permitting, often confused with the more tacit and confusing *acquiescence,* as in: *The nearest of kin, out of financial distress, may acquiesce and use the word "permission" but later regret it, or outright deny such a conversation ever happened.* **See also:** quandary.

Emma woke up thinking about her author's body. At first, it was just that Beatriz had one, a body as female and vulnerable as her own. Yet in the shower, Emma could not help imagining the details until she had fathomed them all, her author fully undressed at thirty-four, the age she herself was now. She imagined Beatriz looking down as she scrubbed her arms, considering her breasts and the ribs visible beneath her skin, remembering who had touched her and where, the men all over Rio who had turned to observe her and her green eyes and had no idea what she would go on to write. Who wouldn't have cared if they had known.

In the nearly ten years that Emma had spent translating Beatriz, it had never occurred to her to consider whether her author's body possessed as many complicated secrets as her fiction did. But why wouldn't it? Wouldn't it have to?

On her first read through the pages from Raquel, Emma kept skipping ahead. The shadow figure lurking in the alley behind the cinema felt so uncharacteristically contrived, a device out of a Sue Grafton murder mystery—*S Is for Shadow*. She kept waiting for Beatriz to subvert the cliché.

Yet every retelling led to the same stock image of a shadow and stopped. In the other scene, in Salvador, Beatriz kept losing traction, too. As Emma read on, she began to squirm. Any of the father's averted-disaster tales could've veered into the stranger, more fantastical territory that Beatriz was known for, but none of them did. She'd never read anything from Beatriz so relentlessly flat and void of magic.

Unless, perhaps, the relentlessness was the point. Still, by the tenth iteration, Emma felt so exasperated with the alley scene that she had to put the pages down. When Raquel had been hesitant to hand her the manuscript, Emma had assumed it had to do with how little Raquel trusted or even tolerated her. But surely Raquel's hesitation had come as much, if not more, from a mistrust of the pages themselves and what they possibly revealed.

If the scenes were from Beatriz's own life, Emma wondered what had happened first. If it was the writing about those minutes in the alley that had sent her author impulsively clicking her way into hundreds of thousands of dollars in poker debt. Or if the poker problem had happened first, and, unable to focus on her writing, Beatriz had gone back to her early journals to revisit what they contained.

Or maybe it had been more complicated. Maybe what had unmoored Beatriz was not just revisiting that alley in her mind but her incapacity to move beyond the facts of the scene for the sake of story, to take the sort of imaginative, magical leaps that people — Emma included — had come to expect. She stiffened at the thought of all the adoring emails she'd sent Beatriz over the past year, how much she'd gushed about her eagerness to get lost in the wonderful strangeness of Beatriz's new book when it was finished.

In her classes at Pitt, Emma had often spoken of her friendship with her author, how well they'd come to know each other. On her trips to Rio, she'd told Beatriz more about her boredom with Miles than she had any of her friends in Pittsburgh. Although perhaps those confidences had as much to do with being a visitor in Portuguese as it did with Beatriz. It had been so much easier to say that there was something deadening about running alongside Miles when she was speaking in another language and with a lilt and leaving in seven days. In response to this confidence, Beatriz had brought up a poem by Hilda Hilst, a wonderful line about a woman unwilling to keep to the room where her lover wanted her to remain. The line had tendered as much understanding, or more, as any reciprocal confession.

Or no, maybe it hadn't happened that way. Recalling the conversation now, Emma wasn't sure if it had been Beatriz who'd brought up the Hilst poem, or if she herself had, and Beatriz had just gone on sitting there, listening.

Emma pushed aside her author's unfinished manuscript and pressed open her notebook against the bed. A jolt of words came to her, as if she'd just touched an electric fence, the sentences coming too fast to second-guess them. On the stand, the hazy specter of every translator ever put on trial rose and requested a mirror. For wasn't it time for the eternal translator to be provided with an aid in the defense of her alleged crimes? At this late point in human history, didn't anyone being tried for literary offenses have a right, even an obligation, to show the spectators in the gallery their own reflections as they watched her and what power their expressions had over her own?

THUMP THUMP!

THUMP THUMP THUMP!

Emma jumped up from where she'd been hunched over her notebook. She'd been so focused that she'd forgotten where she was. The person at the door banged again, rattling the frame of the watercolor beach scene hanging above the bed. They had come for her. She was going to die here. Raquel had been right.

Emma had made it a habit to fasten the chain lock on the door every time she returned to her hotel room, but maybe it wouldn't matter. She'd seen hit men in movies tear the chain lock off its track as if it were no more than a string of cheap pearls around a woman's neck. If she didn't answer her phone or her email, she wondered if it would occur to Raquel or Marcus to call the U.S. Embassy. If they would know how to reach her parents. She thought of her mother, asleep on the plaid sofa, getting such a call but it was too awful. Impossible.

Hey, it's Marcus, the thumper said. Open up.

Emma didn't reply. It sounded like Marcus, but that didn't mean it couldn't be someone else, a hit man with a talent for imitation. She reached for her laptop and clicked on the last message from Miles. He checked his email incessantly in the evenings.

THUMP! THUMP!

Emma, *você está aí?*

How do I know you're really Marcus? she called through the door as she typed.

Because I brought your wet sneakers into your room so you'd have sex with me.

And how long did I let you stay?

Not long enough, the voice on the other side answered. You were writing.

She unlatched the lock. The harsh fluorescent lighting of hotel hallways usually robbed a face of its beauty, but not Marcus's. Not his high cheekbones and full mouth or his radioactive-green eyes. Emma pulled the door shut and he ran his hands over the goose bumps on her arms, over her breasts and down her ribs.

She didn't ask if he'd called Raquel or if he knew that he might be kidnapped and lose an ear at any moment. What would it help if he knew now? He'd just arrived and they'd locked the door. She'd spent her life desperate to measure exactly how much she knew, and what had it gotten her?

A PhD.

An adjunct teaching job that came with a rusted metal desk she had to share with two other adjuncts, one of whom lived on Doritos and left neon-orange fingerprints on her Post-its.

A boyfriend who spent his evenings charting how his pulse rose during his morning run.

Outside the window of Emma's hotel room, the Bahian moon was blue tinged and full over the ocean. Somebody on the street kept shouting, Maria, *por favor!* Come back here. Farther off, a car backfired, or it was a bullet shooting starlike through the dark. In her room, the thermostat glowed the temperature in Celsius. A balmy 31 degrees.

To: eneufeld@pitt.edu
Subject: Re: if you don't hear from me
tomorrow

Emma, your email was incoherent. Whose
ear are you talking about? You need to
get up RIGHT NOW and take a cab to
the American embassy. The address is at
brazil.usembassy.gov. I can't get to
Salvador until 9:23 tomorrow night.

Did you click on the link yet?
brazil.usembassy.gov. GO NOW. This writer,
her children—they are strangers. What
you're doing down there is not your life.

For breakfast, they ordered omelets and slices of guava. When room service knocked, Marcus wrapped a towel around his waist and sauntered to the door with the ease of someone who was not unaccustomed to receiving his breakfast in this manner.

When she woke earlier, Emma had given in to the impulse to check her email while Marcus slept on beside her. She'd tried for a few minutes to just lie there, half-dozing, listening to the rattle of vendors' carts assembling along the beach. She was sorry she hadn't tried a little longer. Having seen her email, there was no postponing her dread of reckoning with Miles.

Unless she was willing to be cruel and switch hotels.

Divino! Marcus exclaimed over the toast, wiping some crumbs from his mouth. He reached down into his backpack lying open beside the bed and Emma assumed he was reaching for another condom, but he pulled out the new edition of *Have You Tasted the Butterflies.*

Did you see this at the airport? I've never finished any of my mother's books. He handed Emma the new edition. I knew her books were all in the apartment, but so was she. It never felt right to read her when I could hear her in the next room. Or maybe I wasn't ready to know what she said in them. He shrugged. Or it was just laziness.

Emma touched the book's sleek new cover, its austere fork and knife. Even her author's work had become unfamiliar to her now.

I had no idea so much of it was about adultery, Marcus said.

Well, and also the dream lives of pigeons.

That part I couldn't follow. He pulled the sheet up as if he'd gotten cold. Will you read it? he asked. From the part about the pigeons?

Still naked, her fingertips sticky with guava, Emma began to murmur the words for Marcus that his mother had written before he was born. At first, she spoke the words so softly that she could barely hear herself, and Marcus drew closer.

With each sentence, she sank further into the words and her voice began to rise. She'd lived with these descriptions for so long, had mulled over them as she drove through the snow and while she brushed her teeth.

And wasn't the splendor of translation this very thing—to discover sentences this beautiful and then have the chance to make someone else hear their beauty who had yet to hear it? To arrive, at least once, at a moment this intimate and singular, which would not be possible without these words arranged in this order on this page?

For I know something, she read, about the dream life of pigeons. I know their dreams are not unlike the floating thoughts of a woman who's forgotten herself in a bath. A woman who's willed herself into a slumber as the water streams, steaming, from the faucet over the full tub and onto the floor, slowly leaking into the room below.

I know that pigeons, in their dreams, are also not unlike the willed slumber of the woman's husband, who is in someone else's bed in another part of town. A husband who wants to believe his wife is sleeping soundly in their home, a home he maintains at a distance that is not unlike the distance a pigeon keeps from the meaning of its dreams. Meanings that can be occasionally gathered in the droppings a pigeon may release into the air, the meanings spattered across windshields and tabletops and sometimes on the bald, unsuspecting heads of men.

Ah, that's my mother's there. Marcus pressed his lips to Emma's shoulder and she continued more slowly, more luxuriantly. She'd read an essay by Borges once in which he'd used the word *"lujosamente"* to describe the voice in Joseph Mardrus's translation of *A Thousand and One Nights*.

It is Mardrus's infidelity, Borges declared, Mardrus's happy and creative infidelity that must matter to us.

And matter LUXURIANTLY, she had added in the margin. Miles had been sitting next to her when she was reading the essay and made fun of her for putting the word in all caps like an adolescent girl. That same weekend Elsewhere Press had approached her about translating a second book by Beatriz. When she told Miles that she'd agreed to the project, he'd pursed his lips as if he'd just noticed the green crusted residue of a pea soup in the corners of her mouth.

For months after, at the thought of that moment, she experienced what García Márquez described as poisonous lilies taking root in her entrails.

On top of her now, Marcus ran his tongue along her collarbone. *Segue, tradutora,* he said. Continue.

And so she continued all morning, LUXURIANTLY, until page seventy-six, when the entire building filled with bathwater and pinkish suds spilled over the windowsills and her voice began to crack and her wrists began to wilt from holding up the book and the phone began to ring and ring and she knew it was Raquel and that her author would want her to answer. There was also the matter of Miles closing in.

The news here at Radio Globo, my friends, is grue-
some. We've just heard that the second of our writers
to disappear into the trees of Rio was found castrated
and dead in his car this morning. Vicente Tourinho, a
mere twenty-six years old.

Here at Radio Globo, we shudder for Tourinho. All you
other authors out there in Rio, please, please stay out
of the trees!

Raquel no longer felt safe anywhere. In her hotel room, she couldn't shower without checking for intruders in the empty cabinets under the sinks. She couldn't fall asleep without testing the bolt on the door. And she couldn't remain asleep either. Every few hours, she would wake and tense and have to check for men in the bathroom cabinets again.

Sitting in the shady café garden where she'd told Marcus and Emma to meet her, she felt tired enough to fall asleep at the table. The description of the café online had said that the garden was quiet and secluded, which seemed true enough. Fat-bottomed palm trees framed the perimeter, the pinnate leaves of the taller ones creating a partial roof overhead.

But were a few squatting palms really going to protect them? She was still sitting here alone. Her mother still owed half a million dollars to a psychopath. When her phone rang and she saw that it was Thiago, she was so grateful she began to cry.

Bom dia, fugitive! What's that noise—you're not getting weepy, are you?

Of course not. I'm not a crier. She pressed her hand over her nose to stifle the sound.

You are a menacing machine, *mulher!* he shouted at her from

Rio. This place is a shit show without you. When are you coming back?

I don't know. The loan shark just threatened to kidnap my brother.

You got to love this country, eh? Viva Brazil! Thiago whistled a little samba into the phone. But seriously, woman, you come from Jews—don't your people always have some money in the mattress for crap like this? You're going to prevail, Raquel, you always do. Gotta run. That ass pimple Enrico's calling.

And he was gone.

That was it, all she'd get of him from here.

Before she could wallow or recover, Emma and Marcus came through the door of the café into the back garden. Her brother bent to kiss her first and she didn't bother to berate him for coming to Salvador without telling her or for going straight to Emma's bed. He was like their mother. With their green eyes and quiet, reptilian ways, they did things exactly as they pleased. Watching him sit down across from her, she thought of all the things Marcus had not been, and would never be.

Not the offspring of a shadow.

Not terrified to ask their mother about that shadow and equally terrified that he might never have a chance to ask her.

And Marcus, tall, slinky, jewel-eyed Marcus, was not waking every morning alone.

He was not obliged to stare across this table at their mother's translator, so sated and aglow she might as well have hung a sign around her neck that said I JUST HAD SEX WITH YOUR BROTHER. IT WAS SUBLIME.

While her author's children argued, Emma kept her head lowered and tried her best to be present yet invisible. The table that
the waitress had given them was wobbly, the legs tipping back
and forth every time Marcus or Raquel put their hands on it.
Even a week ago, Emma would have quietly tried to steady it for
them to stop the banging, but she didn't now. Marcus was adamant that they call their relatives in São Paulo, but Raquel said
they wouldn't give that kind of money. She said their mother
hadn't been in touch with them for so long. Marcus tilted the
table and said the alternative was to give Flamenguinho's messages to the media and see if the coverage scared him into backing down, but Raquel told Marcus he was naive. She said the media
made a soap opera of kidnappings all the time and it changed
nothing. The news in Brazil, she said, was run by a bunch of
union-loving idiots. Marcus asked her not to launch into one of
her tirades and she told him to go to hell.

In the tense silence that followed, Emma kept her eyes down and
her hands on her lap. She couldn't think of anything to offer and
knew they were not going to ask anything of her either, which left
her free to panic about Miles landing in Bahia in nine hours. From
there, he'd make his way to her hotel and then to her room. These
were facts she had yet to relay in Portuguese to her author's son.

She heard Marcus push back his chair. Anyone else want a caipirinha? Emma wasn't sure she could stomach alcohol this early in the day but she nodded yes. In Marcus's absence, she became more acutely aware of Raquel's foot or knee, something of hers, tapping frantically against the table leg.

When the breeze sent Emma's napkin sliding toward the edge, Raquel pinned it to the table like a bug. You should've called me the second he arrived, she said. He's my brother.

But it was two in the morning. It was so late.

Did you show him my mother's pages?

I told him about them, but I—

Give me the manuscript.

Raquel snatched it from Emma's hand before she could place it on the table. Let's make something clear, okay? If my mother never surfaces, you can find someone else to cheat on your husband with and some other book to translate. This is my family.

Emma opened her mouth to say that she wasn't married, that she would be devoted to Beatriz's work for the rest of her life, when something happened inside the café. Several large men had entered, their movements so dark and swift it was as if a colony of bats had taken over the entrance.

Something screeched.

Somebody shouted.

By the time Emma and Raquel rushed inside, all that was left of Marcus was a tall glass shipwrecked on the bar in a spill of caipirinha. On the floor, a scatter of ice and lemons.

Rocha summoned a waiter to remove his caipirinha from the table. The lemon rinds were caked with dirt. Outrageous. Didn't the Aram Yamí wash its fruit properly before serving it? Did they have no standards of basic hygiene?

I'm so sorry, sir, the waiter said.

Rocha turned his face away, disgusted, until the offending glass had disappeared. In these few hours left in Salvador before his flight back to Rio, he'd felt increasingly furious with himself. Only a floundering, desperate man would travel all this way to find a writer he hadn't published in twenty years. He'd never been able to cajole Beatriz into doing anything she didn't want to do. No one could. She'd only written to him now for his money. He had no reason to believe she'd give him a manuscript just because he'd paid for her hotels, or that she even had a finished manuscript to give to anyone.

He'd been correct to schedule a flight for this very afternoon. Until then, perhaps he'd take a walk down the street for a box of mints. He needed to do something that bordered on exercise so he wouldn't have to lie to Alessandro when he returned.

In the lobby of the Aram Yamí, he stopped at the reception desk to ask, just one more time, if anyone had stopped by.

Sim, Senhor Roberto, the receptionist said. Two women came by about half an hour ago and asked for you to call them at this number as soon as possible.

The receptionist handed over an envelope with the Aram Yamí's ornate logo on it and a folded-up Post-it inside, with nothing on it but numbers. At last. They'd found Beatriz.

A rubbery feeling filled Emma's head as she reentered the Aram Yami. At the reception desk, she had trouble recalling Rocha's first name and then stuttered as she said her own. Beside her, Raquel was weeping and making frantic calls on her cell. In the elevator, Raquel's phone stopped getting reception, and she clutched Emma's arm like a blind person.

They could be hacking off my brother's ear right now, Raquel said. He could be bleeding to death as we're standing here in this elevator. Maybe they'll leave him in the trunk of a car until he suffocates from the heat.

That's not going to happen, Emma assured her, as if they were speaking about a book she'd been teaching for years. As if there weren't anyone as reliable in a kidnapping as a devoted translator.

The elevator dinged.

Its single wooden panel slid open.

In the blue, carpeted quiet leading to Rocha's room, Emma thought of her own hotel room, of Marcus's clothes waiting for her, draped over the chair and on the desk, of his toothbrush beside the sink, his mother's novel still face down on the page where they had stopped reading it this morning. Of Miles arriving, impossibly, in five and a half hours.

Emma, keep going. It's not that door.

I just need a second.

But Rocha had heard them and stepped out into the hall. It's fine, take a second, he said. Nothing wrong with a little hesitation before hitting up a man for his fortune.

Hesitation: From the Latin *haerere,* to adhere or cling. A delay due to uncertainty of mind, as in: *The translator didn't hesitate before taking on her author's next novel, or before declaring her life's work was to further the recognition of said author, an identity she adhered to until, in a certain hallway, she hesitated.*

Rocha's room was immaculate. He hadn't left a single garment in view, no voluminous pajamas on the bed, not a single sock, not even a pair of shoes on the floor. Besides the bed, the only places to sit down were two stiff, paisley-printed armchairs. Rocha sank into one and Raquel the other. Raquel had been the one to insist that they meet here, in Rocha's room, to be sure no one could eavesdrop. With both chairs occupied, Emma was left hovering slightly to the side of the conversation. It was not an unfamiliar position or one without benefits. Present but unacknowledged, she was under no pressure to speak. This didn't mean she couldn't, however. Or that, timed right, her influence couldn't prove significant, even pivotal.

Raquel, dear, Rocha was saying, if I give you the ransom money, these hyenas will know you've found a source of significant cash. They'll just keep feasting on you for more.

But we'll pay you back eventually. All I'm asking for is a loan. They have my brother, for God's sake. *Puta que o pariu!* Raquel swore, and let out such a primal, sorrowful sound that Emma saw something give in Rocha's face, and she thought, Now.

What if instead of a loan, she spoke up, it was a trade? If in exchange for the ransom we could offer you, Roberto, a new manuscript by Beatriz?

At the word "manuscript," both Raquel and Rocha sat up in their chairs as if a tremor had passed through the room.

I thought she was getting nowhere with the new book, he said.

She has over two hundred pages.

But they're private still, Raquel said. They're just a jumble of scenes. She shot a violent glare at Emma, but Rocha had already turned his rotund body as much as the armchair would allow.

And the manuscript is here, in Salvador? he asked.

It's here in this room, Emma said. If you write the check, you can have it now.

No, he can't, Raquel said, but Emma ignored her. Rocha's face had taken on a hot glow, his eyes flaming in his round face like a pair of candles inside a carved pumpkin.

Obviously, something has to be done for poor Marcus, Rocha said, but seventy-five thousand dollars—

We can take it to Alfaguara or another publisher if you're not interested, Emma said. Raquel let out a huff in the other armchair, but she was the present but unacknowledged one now.

How about fifty? Rocha wagered.

Eighty, Emma said. With all the media attention, the book will sell out immediately.

Rocha sat back in his chair and Emma felt the chips sliding in her direction. She willed her face to stay impassive, willed her thoughts not to return to Marcus happening upon her thigh in the taxi, of him straddling her in bed.

You must be familiar with her vignette "The Old Man and His Book," Rocha said.

I translated it in one night, Emma said. It was a short piece, no more than a few hundred words. An old man got into bed with the only book he'd ever owned and found that a blue fungus had begun to bloom over the words. The man tried to pick off the fungus with his fingernails. He knew the sentences by heart, but he still opened the book for the pleasure of the letters, of seeing them form the words he already knew. Yet the more fungus he scraped off, the bluer his hands became. By the time someone from the village found the old man deceased in his bed, they couldn't tell where the fungus on the pages ended and the old man's blued hands began.

I thought *Para R.* was for Raquel, Emma said, but the story is for you. For your hands.

Rocha reached for the briefcase beside the claw-footed leg of his chair, and Emma realized she was holding her breath.

Oh, yes, he was still breathing. He was still alive. No one was going to seal the coffin on Roberto Rocha and Editora Eco just yet. On the plane, he made so many notes and edits on Beatriz's manuscript that both of his pens ran out of ink and he had to ask the stewardess for another and work with the poorest quality writing utensil imaginable.

The first drafts he'd seen from Beatriz thirty years ago had been just like this, with each burst of brilliance buried in pages and pages of excess and repetitions. The translator had been shrewd to bargain the way she had, but Rocha didn't feel swindled. He'd worked with Beatriz on enough stories to know that something sublime was buried here. It was just a question of streamlining. By the time his plane began its descent toward Galeão International Airport, he'd figured it out: the story was in the changes. All he had to do was winnow out everything but the details that altered in each telling. The beauty of the story was the futility of it, the devastating failure of the author's attempts to recast a rape and its aftermath by simply changing the fabric of a dress or the entrée on the table.

With Beatriz missing, the critics were going to speculate until they got light-headed about whether the scene at Cine Paissandu was autobiographical. Alessandro was going to be horrified at how much he'd paid for the manuscript, but what was money for if not to halt the mutilation of some boy's face and his possible death? What was the point of being an editor if he didn't have a manuscript like this one in front of him, if his days contained nothing but enervating sentences that risked nothing, asked nothing, did nothing but require ink in a book that generated no real emotion, no genuine unease, not even from the editor who published it?

Rocha shook out the last greasy cashew from his in-flight snack mix and crumpled up the bag like so much fiction. With his other hand, he set the milk in his coffee awhirl.

The world, according to Beatriz, made no exceptions for lovers. A flood was just as likely to carry away two devoted lovers in a bed as it was a house filled with cobwebs. A dengue-infected mosquito was just as likely to bite the back of a man kissing his wife as the knee of a politician while he hid the city's coffers in his armoire.

And the world had made no exception for Marcus. Emma had slept with him, read his mother's work to him while he lay so close to her she could hear his heart. None of it had kept him safe. They'd wired Rocha's money to Flamenguinho immediately, but when she returned to her hotel at four, there was a shoe box inside a plastic bag waiting for her at the reception desk. It was an orange shoe box with the Nike logo on top. Inside, someone had placed a note and a sandwich-size plastic bag. Within the bag was a blood-crusted ear she had licked so recently she could still half taste it on her tongue.

The world made no exception for lovers. She had performed the sentence in English, had read it with a great sense of importance on a panel on Luso-Brazilian literature in Minneapolis and at a reading at the Barnes & Noble in Squirrel Hill. To get the sentence just right, she'd murmured it over and over, determined to re-create the spare beauty of its music, its somber tone.

Yet recalling the passage now, she felt numb to its beauty. All that registered was its desolation. She felt it with everything in her that could ache and break down. Because the world did not stop for lovers, Beatriz had written, lovers had no obligation to stop for the world or for the rain, for the beginning of a war or for its end. And there was nothing to be done about the lovers in the room next to Emma's now, the sound of their headboard banging against the wall while she sat here, trembling.

Even mutilated, the shriveled-up flesh of Marcus's ear looked particular, clearly belonging to a singular human form, just as the handwritten note was inexorably human in the inconsistent curves of its letters and the lunacy of its lines:

YOUR LOVER BOY CRIES LIKE
A GIRL.
YOU'RE GOOD FOR
FORTY MORE, TRANSLATOR.
SEND IT BY MIDNIGHT
OR I'LL SEND YOU A CHUNK
OF THE OTHER EAR.
SEND THE MONEY NOW
AND YOU GET YOUR
LOVER BOY
TOMORROW.

Emma translated the note several times, as if there were a chance that if she went over it again she might be able to come up with a less horrifying version, or could modify it so that it would suggest something slightly different, that Marcus was not tied up somewhere crying in pain or already unconscious by now. They must have put something on his head to bandage the wound. If they let him bleed to death or get an infection, there would be no money. She was fairly sure that was how kidnappings worked.

For the first time since she arrived in Brazil, she felt a longing for Pittsburgh, for the alphabetical order of the books above her desk and the plaintive meows of her cats, cries that required no more than a can opener and Fancy Feast to resolve.

She longed for her classroom, for her fastidiously maintained binder of attendance sheets. She even longed for her shared crappy office, to be sitting in a place where passion was nothing more than a conversation, a posturing to be defended behind a desk with a cup of tea.

If Miles cared enough to come here for her, maybe she would be a fool not to return with him. What was she doing here holding this other man's ear? She didn't know if she was in love with Marcus. For now, it didn't matter.

Matter: From the Latin word for the woody part of a tree, derivative of *mater,* mother. **1.** Something that can be perceived by one or more senses—an ear, for example, as seen by an eye. **2.** A subject to which a person may refer without having to name it, as in: *A woman stared at the matter on her lap.*

Emma switched the hotel phone from one ear to the other as she waited for Raquel to respond to the news. Yet however she held the phone, she felt horribly aware of her ears, felt them hotly against her head.

Raquel, are you there? Should I read... Would it be better if... Her grasp of Portuguese felt suddenly, irremediably inadequate. On the other end, she heard water running, sobs, something clattering against the porcelain of a sink.

How much more do they want? Raquel rasped into the phone.

Forty.

Call Rocha.

And you'll call the police?

Fuck the police, Emma! *Ave Maria.* They never find anyone who's kidnapped. They'll just sell the report to the newspapers. Cops get paid shit here. This isn't your country, okay? Do you get that? You don't understand what's going on! Raquel was wailing now and Emma didn't know what else to do but go on listening and staring down into the shoe box at Marcus's ear.

In the next room, the lovers had turned on the shower and the woman was belting out Marisa Monte's "O Que Você Quer Saber de Verdade" in a shrill, prickling falsetto. Emma wished she could ask for them to switch rooms, as she couldn't leave this one. What if Marcus managed to escape and stumbled here, clutching at the bloody wound where his left ear had been? To figure out that it was the left, she'd had to imagine the clotted, withered edge of it against the side of her own face, on which side it would curve in against her head.

You get Rocha, Raquel told her. Call him right now.

Emma said of course, she'd call immediately. When Rocha balked at the amount, she clutched the Nike box against her body with one hand and told him Raquel had reached a deal with Flamenguinho. He originally asked for sixty thousand, she lied, but we told him we could only bring him forty and he said that was enough.

Or that's what he's saying until you send the money.

But he already backed down from what he originally asked for. Her face flushed at her audacity. But what else did she have? Audacious stories were how she had come by her Portuguese. They were what had drawn Rocha all this way to Salvador.

She asked him if he had another suggestion. If he thought it was really an option to just wait for this man to send Marcus's other ear tomorrow.

No, of course not. I'll wire the money to Raquel's account again. I hope you're correct that this is the end of it.

Obrigada. Emma thanked him, hearing the Yankee clang of her accent in a way she hadn't heard it in years. She'd learned the language too late to ever get the *r*'s right. Every time she spoke it was unavoidable: she released a fleet of mistakes.

Two women who disliked each other huddled on the edge of a hotel bed like sisters. For some time, they had been hunched this way over the tiny screen of a phone, waiting for the alert of a new email to appear. While they stared, one of the women thought of a story the other's mother had written. It was about a tribe in which no one looked each other in the eye, believing that such avoidance could ward off the arrival of jaguars. After the occasional animal slunk off with a baby in its jaws, the women would meet in the shade to grind their manioc and lower their heads more intently. They would murmur about the heat, listening for the judgment in the others' voices.

On the edge of the hotel bed, the two women made a similar effort not to look up from the phone if they sensed that the other had just done so. As is the nature of avoided events, it happened anyway. They both looked up at once, their faces so close they had no choice but to stare into the dilated pupils of the other. They saw the loosened skin over each other's eyelids, the creases fixing deeper into the other's brow. They were in their midthirties now and, as at any age, there were jaguars.

They saw this in each other's eyes and looked away.

To: raquel.yagoda@gmail.com.br
Subject: obrigado você

GOT THE MONEY, AMIGA.

I'LL SEND THE ADDRESS FOR THE ALLEY SOON.
SOMEONE WILL MEET YOU THERE TOMORROW
WITH YOUR BROTHER.

YOU CAN COME WITH YOUR PRETTY AMERICAN
BUT NO ONE ELSE. I HAVE CONTACTS YOU
DON'T. CALL THE COPS AND YOU'RE ALL DEAD.

Once again, Raquel found herself having dinner on American time at a sultry 6 p.m. The only Brazilians around them in the restaurant were the waitstaff. All the diners were tourists, many of whom, Raquel found, didn't seem to notice that they kept scraping their forks against their plates. Emma had insisted on this irritating hour on the pretext that she absolutely had to be in bed by eight, and she kept neurotically checking the time.

The way Emma was knocking back the caipirinhas tonight, however, Raquel wasn't sure whether Emma was going to make it to her room. Why don't you try and relax a little? Raquel told her. We've got a meeting scheduled. We've done everything we can.

But what if my lie to Rocha backfires? What if right before we're supposed to meet and get Marcus, they ask for more? It could happen. Emma tipped the rest of her drink into her mouth. At every other meal, Emma had been a sipper, bringing the edge of her glass to her lips as hesitantly as a hummingbird at a feeder. Raquel had found that this inhibited way of sipping diminished some of the pleasure of her own drink. But watching Emma now, gulping down a third caipirinha like a glass of water, was even more disturbing.

Emma, take a breath, would you please? Raquel leaned toward

her over the table. Flamenguinho's going to get his money. We need to act like we trust tomorrow he's going to do what he agreed to. If you're going to be this nervous, you shouldn't come.

To the alley? I have to go with you. It's too risky to show up alone.

Raquel was worried the opposite might be true but didn't say so. It seemed just as likely that having Emma along would mean an extra liability. Before dinner, Raquel had called Thiago for advice. He said that kidnappers in Brazil didn't usually bother with gringos and that he didn't have much patience with the pasty bastards either. He was more concerned for Raquel, he told her, and wanted her to call the cousin of a cousin. He's the Hertz of handguns, Thiago had explained. He rents them by the day. He's got a lady's pistol for you up in Bahia that's as easy to fire as a cigarette lighter.

Raquel asked how much something like that would cost.

Mulher, please. He won't charge you, Thiago told her. The man is family, and he owes me a favor.

Emma stepped into the one clean dress she had left. She put on the filigree earrings she'd picked out online for Miles to buy for her last birthday. She used up her hand cream and trimmed her cuticles, grooming herself like a high school girl because it filled the minutes and she was rather inebriated, but also because she could not decide about Marcus's things, whether to hide them in the closet.

Until now, she'd been stepping around the red snug-fit boxers Marcus had left on the floor. They were still balled up with one of her sweaty unwashed dresses. She had also yet to touch his backpack, which was still open and leaning against the side of the bed. With each hour he'd been missing, his things and how he'd left them had accrued more meaning. She didn't know if she could betray their location for Miles's sake.

In translation, this kind of dilemma was known as domestication. A translator could justify moving around the objects in a sentence if it made it easier for her audience to grasp what was going on. She could even change an object into something more familiar to the reader to avoid baffling him with something he wouldn't understand. It often occurred with food—with a fruit, for example, that the reader wasn't likely to recognize and therefore whose sweetness he could not imagine.

The problem with domesticating things this way, however, was the possible misplacement of truth. Emma had made a practice of keeping this dilemma out of mind, of trusting that she was experienced enough now to intuitively know what could be moved and what couldn't—when the location of an object was, in fact, its meaning.

Which is perhaps why she tripped over the boxers and hit her face on the dresser when Miles knocked on the door.

Jesus, Emma, are you all right?

Miles lifted her chin to see where the blood was dripping from, if it was from her forehead or closer to her eye. You smell like a distillery, he said. How much have you been drinking here?

Emma pushed past him into the bathroom, her hand over her face. Even with pressure, there was enough blood to pink the towels and the water pooling in the sink. She didn't feel much pain, although after four caipirinhas she wasn't feeling much of anything.

Let me see it. Miles hovered over her in one of his baggy Adidas T-shirts. He was so much taller and more intentional, so much more determined to be right. She didn't want him to declare the degree of her injury, even if the concern in the set of his mouth was genuine. Or just familiar. Or the familiar thing was more the smell of his aftershave.

It's definitely stopping, he said, but your eye's swelling up. Have you been drinking like this the whole trip? No wonder you've lost all sense of reality.

Miles, please. Just stop. She tried to back away from him but the toilet was right behind her.

But I don't understand what's going on, he said. If you think getting married means we have to have kids right away, we —

Because everything comes down to having children, right? You're just like your mother. You reduce everyone to that one decision. You think you have everyone figured out that way, but you don't. It's just your own toxic righteousness. I can't stand it! She pushed against him, through him, whatever she could do to get out of the bathroom. But he stayed pressed up close to her, denying her accusations, until they were out of the bathroom and had reached the red boxers balled up with her sundress on the floor.

Whose are those?

Marcus's.

Her son's?

Emma watched the muscles around his mouth tighten as he scanned the room, looking for other evidence of her betrayal. And it was there: the open mouth of Marcus's backpack, his green-striped beach pants by the bedside table, one of his sweaty shirts on the floor.

Miles started to bend over and Emma lunged to retrieve the backpack before he could reach into it, but that wasn't what he was after. He grabbed the notebook off the bed and held it up.

Is that prick a writer now, too? he yelled at her. Is that why you're sleeping with him? So he'll let you translate him next? You're fucking pathetic, Emma.

He doesn't write. It's mine. She reached for the notebook but Miles held it higher, out of her reach.

What do you mean, yours? Can't you see you're sabotaging yourself for things you didn't even write? Who even cares about these weird stories? I mean, come on.

With the book still above his head, he flipped to a page and tilted his head up to find something to read back to her. She scrambled onto the bed to grab the notebook but he moved away.

On the bedside table, the hotel phone rang and startled them both. It was Raquel calling with the news that Flamenguinho was going to return Marcus in an hour. If you want to be there, she told Emma, you need to get in a taxi now.

In all the confusion, Emma saw that Miles had lowered the notebook, and she grabbed it. Could you spell the street? she asked Raquel, writing down the street name just below the passage she had been about to finish, the eternal translator raising the mirror the court had finally placed in her hand.

To enter an alley in the dark.

To have to repeat this scenario and tell herself it was not the same. There was not just one way for a woman to enter an alley. She would not be the small gray mouse that meekly surrenders to the jaws of the snake. Thanks to Thiago, this time would be different. If you have to use it, use it, he had told her. The bullets in it aren't traceable.

In her hotel room, Raquel pulled out the gun one last time and felt a comfort at its heaviness. For a second, she gently ran the muzzle along her arm. Blushing, she nestled it back in her purse.

Emma opened the door with her sandals unbuckled. She couldn't bother with the clasps now, not with Miles pushing at the door, telling her if she left the room now it was over.

I came all this way, he said.

She told him she had also come a long way, that she was sorry she had gone in a different direction. She told him she felt ashamed to be doing this to him. They'd run alongside each other for five years, matching each other's breath for the considerable length of their fading industrial city. To breathe that hard next to someone for so great a distance had felt radical. Yet as often occurred with radical endeavors, the runs became oppressive. After a certain point, they stopped laughing and no longer paused to watch the birds on the bridge. They never lingered in bed instead of running, never read to each other. They'd just kept at it, harder, stopping only to hydrate or for an occasional ache. Emma knew she was likely leading herself toward other, more acute miseries, but she couldn't consider them now.

I'm sorry, Miles, I really am, she said one more time as she closed the door from the hallway.

In her absence, Miles didn't know what to do. He thought of the slightly tilted porch in front of their house. Of their mailman, Alton, arriving each day and slipping their catalogs and

177

bills through the slot in their door. Of their cats, restless and lonely, tracking over the growing mound of mail. Emma couldn't mean it. If he could just persuade her to leave here, she would recognize that immediately.

He took out his lens spray and went to work on the smears on her sunglasses. They were in abysmal condition. Some of the smears were so thick he had to rub at them with his fingernail, but he was confident he could scrape them off.

And he did — all but one.

·

The only light in the alley came from the moon. It was just enough to cast a dim glow over the mounds of trash around the Dumpsters. Emma heard a skittering and then a tinny bang but couldn't see what creature had prompted it — the actions of a rat or something much larger. The lumpy heaps reeked of all that ended up in alleys: rotting food and fresh feces, the stenches mixing and becoming increasingly toxic in the heat.

I know you think it's a bad idea, Emma whispered to Raquel, but we could still call the —

Raquel covered Emma's mouth to cut her off and then took her hand. Emma thought Raquel was consoling her until Raquel jammed her fingers into the leather purse she was carrying and Emma felt the metal object inside it.

Oh, God, she said in English, and all the terror she'd been denying in Portuguese released itself inside her. She'd crossed a significant line in coming here. Raquel had given her so many chances to back out, but she just kept implicating herself further, luring Rocha and his money. She'd had to do it for Marcus, but hadn't there been, and there had, also the invitation of it, to walk all the way to the edge for once, to —

Clap!

A door flew open behind the Dumpster to their right. Raquel

clutched Emma's arm as cockroaches streamed into the center of the alley, skittering over Marcus's flip-flops as he staggered out the door. His T-shirt was brown down the front with dried blood and there was something tied over his head. A burlap bag, knotted around his neck with a thin rope.

Raquel ran to him but Emma held back to let them embrace first. Or because she had already seen it, the shadow of the man emerging behind Marcus, his shape growing larger, his arm reaching into the waist of his pants for —

the sickening click
of a trigger

    the first blast and the bag still
    Marcus slipping on the trash
    the wrappers and roaches
    the burlap over his face

    the nature of shadows
    being their lack of detail
    the inability to know precisely how big and near and

Marcus calling

    Raquel twisting in the man's hold

Emma at the wall considering whether to
                If she moved and

If there's a gun on the table
It must go off

      But if the gun is in a purse
      If there are two guns
      And the protagonist is holding neither of them

If the graffiti is red and large
on the opposite wall

LUISA FLAKS YOU WERE THE ONE
THE ONE THE ONE

      Or the wall displayed another name
      Or no name at all   just a web of lines that
                resembled letters
      Her mind filling them in as

Raquel smelled the *bacalaão* on his fingers
        bit down
        into his thick palm

    until her teeth broke the skin
    until she tasted what lay
    beneath his skin
    his blood
        beginning to
and he began to

    she'd never been stunning
    never publicly revered
    but never weak   never hidden
    never crazy

          gone
the man behind her
yanked at her hair
jerked her head back
      if there is a gun in a purse
      its bullets traceable to no one
her finger bent
and the trigger went off

Emma felt the ricochet up through her body, the loudness of the blasts detonating in her head. Yet she was still standing, still pressed against the brick wall, still conscious enough to see Flamenguinho's man pull open the same door and vanish.

Across the alley, a plume of smoke rose from a bag of garbage, releasing burnt specks of plastic and cardboard and a new scatter of roaches. A few meters beyond the burning bag, Marcus was writhing on his back and clutching his leg, and this time Emma did not consider Raquel. She rushed right toward him, but Raquel was already closer and reaching him faster, restrained Emma with her arm, Stay back! she shouted at Emma. I just shot my brother, for God's sake.

But Emma crouched beside Marcus anyway, tried to undo the knot to get the burlap sack off his head but he kept thrashing and the knot was tight. One side of his shorts was blackening with blood and each time he shuddered the blood darkened faster. We need to make him a tourniquet, she said. We can use my tank top. She started to pull it off but Raquel told her to stop.

Just move back, Raquel insisted, pulling a cotton headband from her purse. As she knotted it around Marcus's thigh, Emma felt something along her own leg, and thought she must be imagining it from staring so fearfully at the blood pooling around

Marcus. But then the rat twitched its hairless tail against her hand and she screamed.

I said get back! Raquel yelled again and this time Emma obeyed. When the ambulance arrived and the EMTs poured out, she stayed where she was. Raquel did all the explaining. With so many people speaking at once, Emma could only grasp fragments of what was being said. Metal things kept snapping on the gurney. Someone finally cut off the burlap sack and she saw the swollen, horrible state of Marcus's face before he turned away and Raquel ducked after the EMTs into the ambulance and there was nothing to do but mutely take a step back and watch. Emma knew the distance—how far to retreat to be respectful yet still present. To remain available yet silent. To quietly withdraw until she was flush up against the dirty bricks of the alley wall.

Once again, my friends, Beatriz Yagoda has kicked the *bunda* of Brazilian literature. We may not know where she is, but here at Radio Globo, we've just gotten word that she has a new book coming out, so somebody must know where she's hiding.

The line for a copy is going to be as long as the anaconda and it's going to sell out fast. So do yourselves a favor, my friends: put your shorts on and get to the Travessa bookstore now. Or you could skip the shorts and get there faster, but if you get arrested or assaulted while reading naked on the bus, you are on your own.

All the images had been there. The only thing Rocha had to do was give each one the space it required. Or so he explained to the interviewers from the magazines who had received the galleys of the new book and kept calling, pushing him to reveal where Beatriz was. He had no problem taking a little perverse pleasure in withholding information. There was an art to the elegant evasion of an answer. But when the questions were about the book itself, how much he'd worked on it with Beatriz, he got nervous. He couldn't entirely recall what he'd done with the manuscript on his plane ride back from Salvador. In his mind, there was just the rapture of those hours, the thrill of them, all the way up in the sky with his pen, editing each passage down to its intrinsic perfection.

But even that thrill felt sickening now as he stood in the air-conditioned marble lobby of his building with the package someone had left for him earlier that morning. Inside the package, covered in Bubble Wrap, was the cheapest sort of knife, its blade crusted with blood, and the following note:

BOA TARDE, SUGAR DADDY,
YOU'RE ALMOST THERE.
$200,000 MORE AND I WILL LEAVE YOUR FAGGOT
FRIEND

WITH THE RED BICYCLE
ALONE.

Crushing the note, Rocha trembled. At well over a hundred kilos, it was not something his body did easily, but his legs were shaking beneath him and he could not stop them. Alessandro had warned him that once the book was released it would only be a matter of time before the loan shark figured out where the cash well was, who was dipping the bucket down and bringing it up full. But the loan shark was a brute and an ignorant fool. A loan shark didn't know anything about literature, what an editor might be willing to do for an author who made all the days holed up in an office worth it.

Or it had been he who'd been the ignorant fool, thinking he could buy Marcus's release and then retreat. But it was only the beginning. The preface to who knew how many other abductions—Alessandro this very afternoon, or tomorrow morning, every minute they spent on the street distorted with paranoia.

With Marcus still in the hospital, it seemed cruel to tell Raquel about this new threat. But she was an adult and it was her compulsive mother who had caused all this. The package still in his hand, Rocha reached into his pocket for his cell. The thoughts in his head were coming at such a furious clip that he had to pause and make an effort to focus, to rehearse his own controlled voice in his head.

Roberto here, he said when she answered.

Immediately, Raquel launched into a litany of details: how long it had taken the doctors to drain Marcus's ear and all the blood tests, the various police figures who kept coming by. Some high-level inspector is in with him now, she said, but Marcus is not up to that kind of interrogation, Roberto. I tried to tell the inspector to let him rest. We can't have reporters waiting for him outside the hospital and following us back to Rio. I mean, poor Marcus—

Raquel, it's out of your hands now. You need to work with the police. And who knows? Maybe with all the media attention they'll feel compelled to actually do something. In the meantime, I've received a package with a filthy knife in it. It's crusted with blood I suspect may be your brother's.

In the immaculate glass doors onto Delfim Moreira Avenue, opening onto the posh center of Leblon, he apprehended his broad reflection, how intimately it resembled that of his father, who had mostly ignored him after adolescence, except for initiating a few select conversations each year to remind Roberto that his inclinations would leave him diseased, or at the very least devastated and alone.

He heard Raquel start with her sobbing again on the other end of the phone, and told her he had to go but that he would take care of this. There were ways.

Inspector Lucio de Santos: I can tell you're in no shape for questions, son, but you should know you're actually a lucky guy. You've still got part of the skin there for a new ear. In six months, they'll be able to sew on a new one, no problem. They'll make it from your own rib—did you know that? Ever read about Adam and Eve?

Victim: [no response]

Inspector de Santos: I know I'm a stranger, but you're going to have to give me something. You said you were blindfolded, but wasn't there some point when they took it off?

Victim: When they hacked off my ear. I told you that already.

Inspector de Santos: But what happened then?

Victim: I saw the machete.

Inspector de Santos: So you must have seen the guy holding it, right? Could you identify him in a picture?

Victim: What for? There are always more hit men in Brazil.

Inspector de Santos: Well, we have a system of justice, son, and we are doing the best we can to address—

Victim: I'm tired.

Inspector de Santos: I have no doubt you are, son, but when they were bandaging your ear, maybe you saw—

Victim: They didn't bandage it. They gave me some gauze and a bowl of dirty water and left the room.

Inspector de Santos: And when they came back in?

Victim: I passed out. I told you.

Inspector de Santos: Right. Well, after something like this, it's hard to know whether you really didn't see where you were or don't want to see it again, you know what I'm saying?

Victim: [no response]

Inspector de Santos: Does your mother know what's happened to you?

Victim: [no response]

Inspector de Santos: Do you have any idea where we could find her?

Victim: [no response]

On the pond beside Hospital Aliança da Bahia, a flock of white herons descended petal-like onto the water. It was the second day that Raquel had come to watch them. There was a bench on the other side of the pond, but a thin gray-haired man was already perched there with a book, and the last thing she wanted to do was get any closer to books and the people who bothered with them. When they got back to Rio, everyone she knew was going to be talking about what Rocha had published and — unless he could buy an end to Flamenguinho — the possible kidnapping of his partner.

To get the book printed in two days and into a handful of select stores, Rocha had paid an exorbitant sum. She didn't think the title he'd chosen, *After the Alley*, was what her mother would have selected, but maybe it was better. Her mother's titles had always embarrassed her with their intentional mistakes of the senses: *Have You Tasted the Butterflies*, *The Warm Green Sound of Your Sleeve*. As if her mother thought there was something beautiful about errors and being mistaken. But what was beautiful about accidentally shooting her brother in an alley, or her mother gambling money she didn't have? What was beautiful about the scabbed-over hole on the side of Marcus's head?

She wanted to call Thiago but didn't feel up to hearing his

jokes about her aim. Across the pond, the old man on the bench was hunched intently over his book, so absorbed that it was as if he had willed his whole being into the pages on his lap. Her mother had read with that kind of abandon. Raquel had never been able to. She'd had too many reservations about giving herself over that way, risking that some book might obliterate her carefully constructed sense of who she was.

Yet a book had done that anyway, and she'd been the one to print it off the computer. She'd put it into Rocha's hands, and now everyone she'd ever met was going to know she wasn't supposed to have happened. How long had it taken her mother to find that error beautiful, or at least the daughter who had come of it?

Raquel reached into her bag for her phone as if the right question might make it ring.

Alessandro had been sleeping beside him for hours, but Rocha was too nervous to sleep. He'd called the two illegal "elimination" services that his sister had insisted upon, though not before she'd berated him for putting their family in such a perilous position over some writer with a gambling problem. He didn't offer an apology and his sister didn't demand one. They were not that sort of family, though she was right that he had gone too far with this. His misstep had been with the translator in his hotel. When she told him Beatriz's new manuscript was there in the room, he'd panted for it like a dog. He'd acted with as little forethought as an animal. Now his name, the love of his life, the full extent of his holdings — it was all exposed.

Disgusted, he got up and shuffled into the kitchen. It was almost dawn. Agitated, he flipped again through the unopened mail from the day before and stopped at a slender blue envelope that he hadn't noted earlier among the bills. The post office stamp said Boipeba, the smallest of the Tinharé islands off the coast of Salvador. It was the slip of island where *After the Alley* ended — or rather where the novel ended in his version of it. The scene he'd chosen for the final page hadn't been the last one in the document, but he'd felt confident that it was the correct place to close the story, and that Beatriz would agree. He'd left the woman standing at the edge of the ocean with her child while the man who is not the child's father lies asleep, oblivious, in the hotel, the sun reflecting so harshly off the sand that the woman tells the little girl to close her eyes.

He'd been uncertain about eliminating the pages after that without Beatriz's permission. At the thought of it now, he nervously jerked back his thumb and sliced it along the edge of the envelope. That damned woman. Whatever she wanted from him now, he would ignore it.

Unfolding the letter inside, he skipped to the end of the message, to the name Yolanda. They had disagreed about that early story as well. He had thought Beatriz could get away with only so many tales of self-sabotage in one book, and Yolanda was an adolescent character. He found teenagers even more irritating in fiction than they tended to be in reality. Yolanda in her foolish adolescent pursuit of gloom pretended to be deaf. She gave herself over to this false malady so completely that she didn't hear, or refused to hear, the soldiers approaching her family's house, or her father calling for her to run and hide in the silo. She just kept cutting things out of her mother's magazines, the word "shine" and then a sliver of a windowpane, her hand guiding the scissor blades as delicately as if she were cutting a bandage off a wound.

Querido Roberto,
The quiet here is complete.
You were right, this was the place to let things end.
Please tell Raquel I'll wait for her.
I'm at the hotel with the yellow umbrellas.

Yolanda

At 4 a.m., Emma entered her room to find Miles snoring in her bed and Marcus's boxers in the trash can. The location of the boxers was easy enough to alter. She just quietly extracted them from the garbage and zipped them into the inner pocket of her luggage.

Miles's current location, however, was harder to resolve, and she was exhausted. So many hours of keeping vigil outside the trauma ward, waiting for news about Marcus, had worn her down. Every time a new nurse appeared, she'd asked for an update and for the woman to let Raquel know she was still there. The nurses had all nodded politely. One had finally given in and told her that Marcus was no longer in danger of dying. Finally, at close to dawn, Raquel had emerged. There'd been two surgeries and a blood transfusion, but he was alive and being pumped with antibiotics through an IV. Most likely, he would be asleep until noon. Raquel insisted that there was no reason for Emma to stay, and so Emma had returned, exhausted, to her hotel though everything in her body told her it was not where she was supposed to be.

For so long, she'd willfully sought the in-between. She'd thought of herself as fated to live suspended, floating between two countries, in the vapor between languages. But too much vaporous freedom brought its own constraints. She now felt as confined by her floating state as other, more wholesome people were to the towns where they were born.

She stared at the man snoring in her bed. She'd gotten under the covers next to him so many times, but her legs would not allow it now. They were already backing up to the door. In the hall, just outside the room, she sank to the floor. The carpet beneath her had the stiff, prickly feel of Astroturf. But what alternative did she have? She couldn't pay for a second room. Her checking account was down to the triple digits, and really, all she needed was to be horizontal for a moment, to lie in this hallway and close her eyes for just a second and continue the scene she hadn't finished in her notebook. In the evening light, the translator's hazy specter on the stand had taken on slightly more definition, if only from the extra lights in the courtroom. All she needed to build her case now was for her author to arrive and testify on her behalf, to tell the court...

Senhora, você precisa de um médico? Você caiu?

Emma woke up to somebody's high-heeled sandals in front of her face. Stiff bristles of grass had imprinted themselves on her cheek and legs. Or no, it wasn't grass. It was carpet. She was still in the hallway. Looking up, she saw that the sandals belonged to a kind-faced older woman with a São Paulo accent. The woman inquired about the cut above her eye and asked if she should call a doctor.

Thank you, but I'm fine, really. Emma tried to get up to demonstrate that she was neither ill nor insane, but one of her feet had turned into a sandbag.

I'm so sorry, she said as the woman helped her to her feet. This is my room, right here. Emma gave a brisk, confident knock to prove it.

Miles swung open the door immediately, already dressed and shaved and freshly furious. You look awful, he said. Where have you been?

I've been nowhere, she replied. Absolutely nowhere.

Then it was noon. The brightest, sight-obliterating Brazilian kind of noon. Emma's eyes were still adjusting as she entered the trauma ward and finally approached Marcus's bed. It took her a minute to comprehend the ruin of swollen skin and stitches that had replaced his face. The misshapen right side of his jaw was now a wedge of raw meat.

Close the door, Raquel ordered from the chair.

Emma obeyed, relieved to have a reason to look away from Marcus and busy herself with the things she'd brought for him. Should I put your clothes here, on the table? I also brought your chocolate and some mango for—

He's in pain, Raquel said. Can you just sit down?

Of course. I'm sorry. Emma clutched her tote bag to her chest, but once again there was no obvious spot for her to put herself. There was only one chair and Raquel was in it. Maybe I should come back later, she offered.

No, now's fine. I really need to eat. Raquel stood up and the two women silently changed places, Emma taking up the lone chair on the far side of the bed, away from the IV stand. Once Raquel had gone, she pressed her lips to Marcus's fingers. His arm looked paler to her now, the veins more visible at the surface.

Minha tradutora, he murmured, and she told him how long she'd sat out in the waiting room, how much she'd wanted to go in the ambulance, but his sister . . .

I know. He closed his eyes. She was now close enough to see the scabs at the corners of his lips, the long row of stitches along the swollen flap that was the remaining gesture of his ear. She felt sick at the savagery of it and at the thought of her author knowing this had happened to her son. Or not knowing.

I'm going to find her for you, she said.

Please don't, and Raquel shouldn't either. We were naive, Marcus said with a tone that was the closest to bitter she'd ever heard from him. We should've gone into hiding like my mother did, or just left the country right away.

Emma felt her heart lurch. Would you leave now? she asked, but Marcus shrugged.

There's no point, he said. They already ravaged me. I'm a man without an ear.

At the mention of the ear, he retracted his hand from under Emma's and closed his eyes. Every consolation she could think of felt inadequate, so she said nothing. She wasn't even sure where to look. Certainly not at his bandaged ear, and not at his neck, which was collared in awful, raw-looking blisters where the rope had held the bag tight around his skin.

And the book, Marcus said with his eyes still closed. Did you bring it with you?

I did. She reached for her bag. I didn't know if you'd want to hear your mother's—

I meant yours. What you've been writing.

Emma leaned into him as if they were on the ferry again with a damp wind against her back. When Marcus leaned to meet her mouth, something beeped on the machines. Must be the libido reader, Marcus said, but the beeping didn't stop. It got faster and shriller. Marcus kissed her harder, and Emma shifted her weight to her wrists, bracing for whoever would enter to attend to the machines and find her there, leaning too far over the bed to pull away.

Another poor *rapaz* from Minas, my friends, is locked up for good. In record time, the police say they have the man who kidnapped Yagoda's son. But the poor *rapaz* they picked up can't write his own name. Here at Radio Globo, we're wondering how he wrote the ransom notes. Would a loan shark with serious cash have a record of stealing gasoline?

And so, my friends, the great circus of Brazilian justice goes on.

The arrest played on the morning news while Raquel sat on her hotel bed. She was finishing off the soggy remains of a sandwich from the hospital cafeteria while she texted Thiago. If she did at least three tasks at once, she felt less conscious about eating so many meals this way, alone.

Do you think that man, she texted Thiago, could kidnap the rice and beans off his own plate?

She swallowed a bit more of her soggy sandwich and reread the message, regretting having sent it. Since the gun, Thiago had offered so little. He took hours to respond, and when he did, the only jokes he made were about giving her job to Enrico if she stayed away much longer—Enrico, who was so cocky and inept they'd spent entire meals making fun of him.

The police believe this arrest may lead to the return of beloved writer Beatriz Yagoda, the newscaster announced, brushing her bleached bangs out of her face, and Raquel clicked off the TV. She also kicked the remote to the floor, then her phone, which made for several desperate seconds of searching when it began to ring.

It was only Rocha, however. In his standard aloof voice, he reported that he'd received a letter from her mother postmarked from the remote island Boipeba. Her request, he said, is for you to go to her.

Raquel looked down at her filthy clothes on the floor, her tank tops wilted with sweat, her yellowed bras. The one well-cut linen dress she'd brought was now stained in two places, though she'd continued to wear it anyhow. She'd even begun reusing her underwear.

Rocha explained that the letter had been very brief, and Raquel nodded, not aware that she'd begun to cry until she wiped her face. And my mother thinks, she said, that she can just send a note through you and I'll jump on the next ferry to Boipeba?

My dear, you are free to do with this information as you please.

Am I? I don't feel particularly free. Raquel yanked open the desk drawer to get the notepad she'd seen there. What's the name of her hotel?

Well, I had my assistant look into the matter and I think you might find her at Pousada do Sol. Your mother's only remark was that she was lodging at the one with yellow umbrellas.

All she gave was the color of the umbrellas? *Puta que o pariu!* Raquel sank onto the bed. She knew this was just the sort of outburst that a man like Rocha would recoil from and she should calm down. He was their only savior.

And what am I supposed to do about my brother? she yelled anyway. Leave my mother's translator in charge? Emma doesn't understand anything about Brazilian hospitals.

The translator will be adequate, Rocha said. I really have to go, dear. *Um beijo.*

Alone again with the little that remained of her soggy hospital sandwich, Raquel turned to her phone to cope in the way of her generation. She tapped the screen and began to search for things.

There was a catamaran to Morro de São Paulo. Then she'd have to take a speedboat. There didn't seem to be a direct route, but with her mother there never had been.

She scrolled down for the boat schedule but found only a single time: one chance a day at 10 a.m.

She had fifty-three minutes.

Chance: From the Latin *cadentia,* that which falls out. **1.** A force assumed to cause events that can neither be foreseen nor controlled, as in: *She could find her mother only by chance and a yellow umbrella.* **2.** A fleeting, favorable set of circumstances. **See also:** gamble, hazard.

The boat's horn was sounding when she arrived, the motor already chopping at the water. Raquel called down the dock for the ticket man to wait, the wheels of her suitcase stuttering over the planks. He gestured for her to take her time, that she was fine, but once she started to run she couldn't stop. She was still panting as he lifted her luggage onto the boat and told her to relax. She wasn't the last one. A man had gotten out of a taxi just behind hers.

Pulled up right after you, the ticket man said.

And he's coming down the dock now? Raquel felt her throat closing. He's followed me, she said. I'll give you forty *reais* if you lift the plank now. Please. She reached for his thin, veiny arm. He was an old man, his eyebrows white and bushy, the skin folding in around his mouth. My ex-boyfriend is terribly violent, she said, scraping around in her wallet for cash.

She held out sixty *reais* and he said, *Está bom, menina,* already lifting the ramp.

As they pulled away, she didn't let herself look. With a face, he would only haunt her longer. She thought of her mother's pages and wondered if her mother had been able to keep her eyes shut. Alongside the catamaran, the blunt edge of the dock was behind them.

They were onto the water now and on their way.

Although he lived in front of the ocean, Rocha did not stop to watch it. To do so had come to feel like a cliché. Yet this morning, he could not resist. And so ten steps behind him the temporary bodyguard he'd hired for himself and Alessandro stopped as well. To be followed all day in this manner was exasperating, but until the services he'd paid for were completed, he had no choice. He had taken his free movement for granted.

He had also forgotten this splendid breeze, how one couldn't feel it without coming to a stop completely, although it was not really the ocean that he was considering now so much as Raquel moving across it, how long it would take her to reach Boipeba. He found her a rather tiresome young woman, but imagining her alone on some boat full of tourists, he felt an ache for her.

Even if she did find her mother, the conversation, or lack of it, would be excruciating. Beatriz would fix her gaze on some gloomy incongruity on the beach—a plastic spoon jutting out of the sand, the hand of a broken doll, some dying bird. Raquel would see her mother looking away and would want more, much more, and who could blame her? Didn't he want more from Beatriz? Didn't everyone?

Miles remained. Emma hadn't had the nerve to kick him out of her room but she hadn't ceded either. The only meal they ate together was breakfast. After that, she left for the hospital and Miles swam endless laps in the hotel pool or took runs when it was still hot enough to sear the skin on his forehead and the tips of his large ears. When Emma brought up the benefits of a hat to him at breakfast, how she'd resisted the idea as well, Miles turned away to scowl at their waiter. He said he could see the man in the doorway doing nothing but staring out at the ocean. This must be why you feel so at home here, he said. Nobody seems to care who might be waiting for them.

Emma responded with a tense smile. It seemed as awkward a time as any to let him know that Marcus was going to be released soon from the hospital. At the news, Miles began chopping at various invisible objects on the table with his butter knife. You can't go on pretending this is your life, he said.

It's been my life for years.

Chop, chop, chop went his knife against the table. A child came by selling flowers made of lacquered shells, and then their waiter crept up to say there would be no espresso today, unfortunately. Something was wrong with the machine. Could he offer them some tea?

The water around the island of Boipeba hid nothing. As the catamaran slowed and docked, Raquel could see clear to the bottom,
all the broken shells spiraling in the wake of the boat, even the
tiny fish glinting among the reeds. Up on the bank, everything
was a blur of tourism. She tried to focus on the hotels and their
umbrellas but was distracted by all the donkeys and foreigners,
the islanders hustling back and forth, trying to make a buck.

Senhora, a bagagem! a man loading up one of the donkeys
shouted, pointing at the waste his animal had just left and
through which she'd just wheeled her luggage.

All week, João had been watching the heavy older woman with the trench coat. It hadn't rained a single day on Boipeba but the woman kept the coat with her at all times, like a purse or a pet. When she first walked into the hotel, he'd assumed with her pale skin and light eyes that she must be a foreigner. But she spoke perfect Carioca Portuguese and didn't ask about air-conditioning or Wi-Fi or any of the things the foreigners wanted to know. She'd just asked for the weekly rate, lit a long Dannemann cigar as if it was the most obvious thing for a heavyset older woman holding a trench coat to do on a remote island, and followed him so quietly to the room that he wouldn't have known she was still behind him if it wasn't for the leafy aroma of her lit cigar.

Every day since then, she had smoked through the afternoons. She'd pick a spot out under the umbrellas or at one of the shaded wooden tables under the palms. Ana, who made up the rooms in the mornings, was the one who first started calling her the Widow Yolanda and said the cigars must have belonged to her husband. João had never seen a woman smoke a cigar in public like that, but then his mother had done strange things after the fishing boat came back without his father. There had been the baths in the middle of the night and, as with the Widow

Yolanda, hours when all his mother could do was stare at the trash can or a crack in the wall as if it were as hypnotizing as the waves.

Mario, the owner, who had been to Rio many times, said he could tell that the widow had been a looker once. He said it was a shame she'd let herself get so round and morose. He said Cariocas were known for staying sexy into their fifties, and with her green eyes and reddish-gray hair, Yolanda would have found a second husband, no problem, if she'd kept herself together.

On the island, however, the Widow Yolanda was most definitely falling apart. Every morning she looked more broken. Her second day on the island she left her lunch uneaten. Her third day she sat on her glasses and cracked one of the lenses. She'd asked João for some tape to hold the frames together enough to wear, though she admitted that she could barely see through the lenses now at all.

When a young woman walked in during breakfast on Friday morning and said Mamãe and ran to the widow, all the guests eating at the other tables turned to watch.

At the daughter's touch, a twitch rippled through the widow as if she were a just-slit eel. João knew he should look away but he couldn't. No one did. The daughter touched her mother's crooked glasses and the filthy trench coat and started sobbing. Next to the daughter, who was not beautiful, he saw what Mario had been talking about. It wasn't just that the daughter didn't have her mother's green eyes or long, slender, foreign-looking nose. When the widow moved, it felt historic. It was like watching an aging leopard slink through a forest. They'd all been mesmerized, trying to imagine how effortlessly she must have hunted once.

And then the Widow Yolanda abruptly let her daughter go and

stepped backward—leaving her daughter's arms out in the air around nothing, in front of everyone. The daughter turned her face as if she'd been struck, and João turned away as well, ashamed for her. There was also, suddenly, a strong smell of fresh dung.

When he looked back, the daughter was stepping out of the breakfast area, the widow behind her. The rest of the day the two of them kept their distance from the hotel. He saw them once on the beach, the widow puffing on one of her long Dannemann cigars, the sleeves of her coat rolled up over her freckled wrists, and the daughter talking, always talking. The next two mornings at breakfast they sat at the farthest table. João couldn't hear what they were saying, though it was the daughter who kept gesturing, squeezing her hands into fists. The Widow Yolanda remained still as a leopard, smoking, listening.

That afternoon, as abruptly as the daughter had appeared, she wheeled her luggage back down to the dock. The widow followed slowly behind her, holding nothing but the coat. They hadn't handed in the key or paid for the last two nights. João knew it was his job to run after a guest in such a situation. It was so awkward. He hated it and couldn't bring himself to do it now, not to the widow and her homely daughter. If Mario gave him a hard time he could just say he didn't see them leave, that they had been sneaky. Mario had said the widow was a Jew.

But Yolanda didn't go. When the boat left, only the daughter was on it. The widow stayed on the dock, watching, the donkeys moving slowly around her. She was still there after the arriving passengers had gone and after the boatmen had left for lunch, the sun beating down on her round, sad shape, and João wondered if he should guide her into the shade, if someone should, but no one did. She wasn't that kind of woman.

To stand on a dock among packs of donkeys and watch your daughter float across the water, away from you.

To watch her through broken, splintered glasses.

To have stayed awake for two nights watching your grown child sleep, a child who you'd forced too early to be an adult and who'd grown thick from it the way a vine will.

To study the woman this child has become as she sleeps heavily next to you.

To drink her in and in, like a stew for which there is no spoon.

To see enough through the fractured glass in your lens to know even in her sleep she is uneasy with you now, abhors the heavy coat you found on a bench which is hideous but you can't let go of it for its pockets.

To fill those wonderful pockets with all the German cigars in Brazil.

To smoke them all.

To work up the nerve slowly,

                  smoking,

        to say it.

To tell your daughter about the blood that ran down your legs and stained your sandals in a restaurant bathroom just after you married her father.

To leave out for your daughter the brief interval of time between the bleeding in the restaurant you called a miscarriage and when you felt pregnant again, to tell her you wrote the sequence the way you did for the sake of story.

To speak of this bleeding to her and then retreat into adages about craft and beauty.

To make no mention of the truth about the interval, that it had been less than a day and the doctor said it was the same pregnancy, that it had been spotting, not a miscarriage, because you were certain he was wrong—it was another baby now and you had chosen the father.

To hold on to this certainty the way one holds on to a coat or a word.

To have made a coat of words and cloaked yourself in it.

To have lifted yourself into an almond tree.

To have climbed higher and higher as you had as a child and recall the same breeze carrying the same scent of almonds, and before you could fall there was your father below, waiting to catch you.

To endure the fact that you were on an island, doing nothing but smoking, while one of your children's ears was delivered to a hotel in a box.

To know the self-loathing that is having brought harm to your son, to both of your children, to have nothing to hide in from this loathing but the dirty coat again.

To hear your daughter say it has the odor of a stranger.

To be this stranger she speaks of.

To find that being a stranger to her all day is like having a fever, your skin burning with it, and meanwhile your daughter seething, unable to bear you.

To watch her leave on a boat through glasses you sat on and which you can't fix in this place where you've heard them call you Widow.

To glimpse now, as she goes, just enough splinters of your daughter through these broken glasses to know.

To wager that her boat has become a hyphen against the water, a comma, and then

By the time Rocha clicked to the right channel he'd missed the
last of the flames. All the cameras were showing now was the
ash, blowing in gusts like swarms of locusts, or like something
more minuscule that couldn't be captured on TV — clusters of
atoms or electrons, the spectral bits of a mind too extraordinary
to leave the world in the ordinary way of simply getting old and
waiting for disease.

Then, at last, the camera zoomed out and he saw the hotel sign
and the yellow umbrellas, how much of the back half of the building had been blackened into a cavity of ashes. A young man from
the island who worked at the reception desk was speaking into a
microphone, but Rocha put him on mute. He couldn't stand to
hear the analysis of some bellhop in flip-flops. He'd already heard
the island people going on about her odd cigars, how the fire had
surely been an accident. But Beatriz had told him and he'd missed
it. She'd said the island was the right place to end and he'd read the
sentence only as it pertained to him and the book of hers he'd published, as her gracious way of letting him know she was not
appalled by what he had done with her pages. He'd read the note
only for what it said about his skill, his worth to her as an editor.

Even now, watching the brigade of shirtless men from the
island splashing buckets of water at the room in which she'd

caught on fire, Rocha could not think of her actual body. Only of her sentences, of Luisa Flaks in the bathtub letting the suds and water flow over the edge and on and on, of how Beatriz had insisted that he misunderstood, that language was what had to be restrained, not the woman she'd invented, not the water pushing over the edge, onto the floor.

And now even the ash was unclear. A speck of soot or sand had gotten stuck on the camera lens, or a smear of water.

Goddamn it, fix it! Rocha shouted at the TV like an old man. But the smudge remained.

Eliminated. That was the word the service had used when they called to let him know that the loan shark was finally gone. They had found him. Rocha's sister had insisted that he hire two services, as one was sure to be incompetent. To pay multiple criminals to find and kill someone on his behalf, to condone a murder, to write a check for one, had made Rocha feel morally loathsome. He'd always thought of himself as more principled than his siblings. He'd indulged himself as they had, but had thought he was different, that when it really mattered he would stick to his principles in a way that his complacent brothers and sisters never would. But it wasn't true. When Marcus was kidnapped, Alessandro had suggested the possibility of hiring a hit man, but Rocha had chafed at the suggestion. Hire a murderer? Endorse such an industry? He'd told Alessandro that the country would never move forward if law-abiding citizens made a practice of hiring murderers to kill one another.

But he had done it. He'd hired a murderer. Several of them. He was a man who kept to his principles at the expense of other people's lives but not his own. Not his lover's. And now there was nothing to do but watch this worthless, sooty footage of a burning building on the TV along with everyone else.

As the boat rose, Raquel held on, clinging to the railing with everyone else. After each wave, the nose of the boat smacked down with such violence they all crashed against their seats. You know the moon is the reason, an older woman clenching the railing next to Raquel said. The woman began to describe her last boat to the mainland just before a full moon and Raquel nodded politely, only half listening, as she didn't plan on taking another boat to Boipeba after this one. She wouldn't be abandoning her exactly. She would just send Marcus instead. He would be able to stand seeing their mother carrying around that dirty coat like a homeless person. She'd send along a new pair of glasses and some fresh clothes and sandals. He would come and decide when it was safe to bring their mother home. It was his turn to make the call. Raquel didn't want to do it again, not this time.

Look at that! The chatty woman beside her pointed to what looked like another jagged wave until Raquel saw it, a long gray line breaking the surface of the water — the tremendous back of a whale.

Then, just as suddenly as it had risen, it sank again.

João wasn't hungry.

But his mother had made him coconut bread and insisted.

So he ate for her.

And his mother hovered, brushing the cinder from his hair.

Emma was extracting hair from her brush in the bathroom when she heard Miles on the other side of the door shouting something about Beatriz. She clicked on the bathroom fan to drown out the sound of his voice. Despite her efforts to be frank with him, he'd refused to leave Brazil or get another room. On long runs, she had admired Miles's ability to continue at any cost. His determination was contagious, perhaps never more so than now, in Brazil. With Miles unwilling to budge, Emma had decided her only course was to leave herself. There was no shortage of hotels in Salvador. Once the hospital released Marcus this afternoon, they would simply head to another.

This morning, however, she was still confined to this situation and to the sound of Miles shouting outside the bathroom. Even with the fan on, she could hear him saying something about a fire. At the word dead, she couldn't help but pause and put down her hairbrush, placing it next to the soap.

She heard him say burned.

She heard obliterated.

Room down around her.

She heard gone. In the hotel lobby on the TV.

Heard enough that she emerged from the bathroom to find the door of the room ajar and the TV on. On the screen a smoky hole was smoldering where a building had been. Tourists and islanders were crowding together in front of it, coughing in the smoke. A helicopter landed as a message in bold white letters scrolled across the bottom of the TV screen: MISSING WRITER BEATRIZ YAGODA FOUND DEAD IN FIRE ON THE ISLAND OF BOIPEBA.

The message scrolled across a second time, a third, and Emma kept on reading, translating it over and over in her head. She was still fixated on the words replaying at the bottom of the screen when she heard Miles speaking to someone just outside the door.

Emma, can you tell this man he's got the wrong room?

At the sound of her name, Emma finally turned from the news and saw Marcus standing transfixed in the open doorway, watching the TV. She registered what was happening but so had Miles, who seized Marcus's T-shirt with both fists and began to shake him so hard Marcus shouted in pain and tried to cover the bandaged side of his head. Emma yelled at Miles to stop and lunged to pull him off, the news playing on behind them, seeming to get louder, devouring the room and then the hallway as Marcus twisted free, and Emma ran after him, apologizing, and he said, Please. My mother is dead. Please leave me alone.

Whether you're listening or not, my friends, whether a beautiful sentence moves you or leaves you cold, Brazilian literature has lost a piece of its soul today. Beatriz Yagoda may have gambled too much and hid from her own children, but she wrote like the room was on fire, and so it went down. At nine this morning she burned to death in a hotel on Boipeba. The flames, my friends, were started by a cigar left burning in her room. Smokers, take heed.

Emma kept to her hotel room in case Marcus called her back. She'd left him message after message until his voice mail was full. Raquel had called once with the details of the funeral but that was all.

Miles had finally flown back to Pittsburgh.

Her author was gone.

Besides the occasional shout on the street or a few fleeting samba notes from a passing car, nothing broke the impersonal quiet of her hotel room. As the long minutes of the humid afternoon turned into the even longer minutes of evening, she got increasingly restless. She looked up flights online but bought none of them. She went out for food, returned, and still the hours until the funeral dripped by like a leak from a faucet.

It was dark by the time she began flipping through her notebook, trying to make out what she had intended in the sentences she'd scratched out and scribbled again. After all that had happened in the past two days, much of her own handwriting had become mysterious to her.

With her translations, she'd learned to type for long stretches without ever looking at the screen. She'd keep her face turned to Beatriz's book, propped open beside her on the desk, or she'd stare out the window and trust her fingers to key in the words as they occurred to her. When she looked back over what she'd typed, there was a kind of magic in seeing that her hands had indeed accurately translated what had come into her mind into sentences on the screen. There was no reason to believe that her fingers wouldn't comply with a similar kind of magic if the words she was typing up happened to be her own.

And if her fingers failed to comply, if what she wrote wasn't worth typing up, who would ever know? She was alone with all the hours of her life.

Transcribe: From the Latin prefix *trans* + *scribere*. **1.** To write something anew and fully, as with a score of music for a new instrument. **2.** To convert a written work in such a way that it alters the expectations of others and/or oneself, often requiring the abandonment of such expectations entirely. **See also:** transform, transgress, translate.

Rocha arranged the reception, a private one, to follow the larger gathering the Ministry of Culture had put together for the public in the Biblioteca Nacional. For the literati, Rocha ordered a full spread from Antiquarius and spoke with the chef directly to ensure that everything would be impeccable, the best trays of meats and fruits, the most expertly prepared cuts of sashimi, a few salads. He chose the flowers himself, small-mouthed vases of cream-colored lilies, and made sure they were arranged with subtlety, not just shoved in with some ferns and other filler.

Every night before the funeral he had woken up and seen the ashes playing across the ceiling above his bed and across the walls, on the mirror in the bathroom. Beyond the phone calls for the funeral preparations, he had barely spoken. A man who knows how to be silent, Beatriz wrote in her third novel, is a man who knows how to begin.

But begin what? For whom?

○

If João had smelled the fire sooner.

If he had stepped out earlier, seen the smoke blowing over the bougainvillea.

If the hose in the garden had been longer.

If the island had owned a proper fire truck, if Mario had bought an extinguisher, if anyone had had the special fire clothes and mask that made it possible to go in and pull a person out of a flaming room.

If they hadn't used so much bamboo for the chairs and also the dressers.

If they had considered how quickly bamboo lit and could fill up a room with smoke.

If she had stayed longer.

If she had insisted her mother also board the boat.

If she had forced her.

If she had been more forgiving.

If the motor had sputtered.

If she hadn't stared so long at that awful coat.

If she had opened her eyes in the dark and gazed back at her mother.

If she'd admitted how good it felt to lie there and feel her mother present, watching.

If there had been anything left of her mother after the fire.

If the firemen had found even some vestige of her teeth.

If Raquel had turned around and waved again, harder.

If she had called out as the boat drew away, had left her mother curious about what it was she'd shouted from the water.

If the waves had been so strong that they couldn't leave.

If the whale.

If the boat.

If the rain.

If we honor what we can recall by accepting that we cannot change it, the rabbi was saying. Or he was making more sense than that but Emma couldn't follow. Her mind felt blanched and she was uneasy. She kept feeling someone watching her and with an unsettling intensity, the way Beatriz had watched her if Emma was walking toward her from the other side of a room.

But that couldn't be. Her author was dead, ashes. Someone at the funeral just happened to study people with a similarly electric gaze. Emma looked around to see who that person could be, but all the heads around her seemed to be lowered for the Kaddish.

She lowered her head as well and forced herself to focus on the words, though she knew them. *Yit'gadal, v'yitkadash,* she murmured along in Hebrew with the elderly relatives who had arrived early and taken up the entire front row. Raquel had refused to ask any of these older aunts and uncles for the ransom money, but she'd invited them to the funeral, and all of them had come, pulling Raquel and Marcus into their arms like children. Once these elderly aunts and uncles were assembled in the front row, it felt right for them to be there, their gravelly voices forming a chorus for the mourner's prayer.

Emma didn't understand why Raquel's loud and hairy boss

had also filed into the front row. The relatives she understood—
they were the ones who would eventually lie next to Beatriz and
her parents and brother, here in the Jewish communal section of
Cemitério do Cajú. If only they had called them earlier.

If Beatriz had gone to them for money instead of Flamenguinho.

If the brother Beatriz had spoken of visiting in this cemetery
hadn't died at seventeen. If he'd known her as only a sibling can
after so many years.

If Emma had known her at all.

If she'd asked better questions.

If she'd asked fewer.

If she'd sat, just once, with Beatriz on the balcony without
getting so nervous she had to string a new curtain of literary
inquiries between them.

If everyone will please turn to page one hundred and ten.

To page one twenty-three.

If you will please give your attention to Raquel, who has chosen a passage from—

○

If you are familiar with my mother's second novel, you may know this scene. It appears just after the mayors die and the butterflies begin to arrive with duller wings.

For years, Raquel began to read, they came in bright abundance, forming clouds over the riverbank. Tourists would arrive by the boatload to behold them in all their orange and pink-tipped magnificence. But then one mayor was undone in his own bed, the other chopped to pieces, and when the butterflies arrived it was not quite as before. First the orange of their wings deepened to a glistening black. Then the pink along the edges reddened to a muddy brown. They began to arrive in ever more colorless clouds and the tourists would not have it. They called them moths and left bewildered.

Only the locals, she read on, continued to call them butterflies, to hold out their arms for them to flutter against their skin. As for the darkening of their wings, along the Amazon they called it the ink blue of the eyes of infants, of the river at six in the evening in the mist after a monsoon.

Raquel paused to steady her hands so the page would stop trembling. But she had waited a beat too long. She'd lost her place on the page. As she searched for where she'd stopped, it occurred to her how many seconds like this were to come, her mother gone and nowhere left to look for her except in a fog of sentences like this one.

In the mist after a monsoon, Raquel repeated, looking out at the crowd that had come to mourn her mother, all of them watching her, waiting for her to read on. Only when her gaze stopped at the second row did she realize who she was looking for, the one person who would know the degree to which her hands had begun to tremble, and also the next words she needed. Emma mouthed the phrase where Raquel had left off and finding it, Raquel continued, reading well past where she'd originally planned to stop, to show that she could. Then she read on, even further, until it was no longer about anyone at the funeral or even about her mother. It was only about the sentences, her breath matching the give-and-take of the cadence, the rhythm filling her chest, and for the first time in days she did not feel empty.

By the time she sat down next to Marcus, she was breathless. Several aunts leaned over to murmur about how beautifully she'd read and she thanked them, her face wet, until Marcus took her hand and she let herself collapse a little against his shoulder, though there was not much of him to collapse against. He'd become so bony. Beneath his suit, his chest was sunken like a ship, and leaning into him, Raquel could not remember why it had felt so necessary for her brother to be equally alone.

Up at the podium, the rabbi who none of them knew reached the end of the final prayer and the dam gave way. The whole river of mourners began to surge toward them. Raquel told Marcus that they would drown if they didn't head directly to the black sedans Rocha had rented for the procession.

Unless, she said, there's someone you want to ask to ride with us.

Marcus hung his head and said he could think of only one person. I'll ask her, Raquel offered. Just go to the car. We'll meet you there.

The semester began. The stacks of syllabi. A student arrived with his T-shirt on inside out. Another walked in chewing gum with her mouth open and with such vigor it required every muscle in her face.

Only this semester the heat stayed and stayed. The leaves remained on the trees.

After her fifth class, Emma found a small yellow lizard crawling into her coffee cup. The next week, her office door jammed from the humidity and she got stuck inside, knocking on her own door until a passing colleague yanked the knob and freed her. The next morning the rusted knob fell off in her hand.

At the Pontifical Catholic University of Rio de Janeiro, there was little that Emma could predict with any consistency. In that regard, it did not feel at odds with the rest of her life. Her parents kept telling her it wasn't enough, that she couldn't live this way in her thirties, on her own in a dangerous country, teaching for so little money she had to rent a room from some musicologist named Esmeralda.

However, Emma only stayed at Esmeralda's when she was writing. Other nights she stayed with Marcus or they took a bus up the coast. At the present moment, for example, they were sitting in some prongs of palm shade studying an older woman who was not the right size or shape to be Beatriz but who was writing in the sand with her toe, stepping closer to the water with each word. As they watched, the waves began to foam around the woman's ankles yet she kept on composing, wading in and in, her words beginning to dissolve as she wrote them. Surely she would be reasonable and stop when the water met her knees.

And if she didn't? If she kept going?

Already, the bathers on the beach had begun to look around, to wonder who would be the first to get up and approach her, and with what question. As for those who remained under their umbrellas, might this stranger come to haunt them anyway? Might they wake in the night and discover foam around their ankles, to find that they were entering the ocean with this unknown woman in their sleep?

ABOUT THE AUTHOR

Idra Novey has written for the *New York Times,* the *Los Angeles Times, New York*, NPR, and *The Paris Review.* Her award-winning fiction and poetry have been translated into eight languages, and she has translated a number of leading Brazilian writers, most recently Clarice Lispector. Idra Novey has lived in Pennsylvania, Chile, and Brazil and currently lives in Brooklyn. *Ways to Disappear* is her first novel.

Made in the USA
Monee, IL
03 August 2023